MALCOLM ROSE was born in Coventry and began his career as a research scientist. He started writing stories while studying for his DPhil degree in chemistry, as a means of escape from everyday life. He is now a full-time writer best known for his gripping science-based thrillers and forensic crime novels. He has been awarded the Angus Book Award twice and the Lancashire Children's Book of the Year.

For more information about Malcolm Rose visit his website: www.malcolmrose.co.uk

KISS OF DEATH

Malcolm Rose

USBORNE

With thanks to
the students of the After Hours Club,
The Long Eaton School,
for their help in naming this book

First published in the UK in 2006 by Usborne Publishing Ltd., Usborne
House, 83-85 Saffron Hill, London EC1N 8RT, England. www.usborne.com

A CIP catalogue record for this book is available from
the British Library

JFMAMJ ASOND/08   9781409504283   Printed in Great Britain.

The Beginning

Rowland Torre gazed up the silent valley, and his heart froze with fear. The stone arch at the head of the dale was empty again. For the second time, his fiancée was nowhere to be seen.

Every day of the last five months, against his parents' wishes, Rowland had trudged from his home in Stoney Middleton to this spot at the edge of Eyam, to see Emmott Syddall. And every day, Emmott had kept their meetings. Until yesterday. Even when the grassy basin had turned pure white with snow, Rowland had stood near the stream. Emmott had been framed by the stone for a few minutes, and they had waved at each other from a safe distance and smiled. Across the field, they hadn't been able to speak or touch, but at least Rowland had been comforted to see that she was well.

Now his shiver had nothing to do with the weather. He feared the worst for his beloved Emmott.

It was April 1666 and the Derbyshire village had been out of bounds for months, while the Black Death ravaged it. The plague had arrived last September in a box of cloth from London. First the sickness took the tailor's assistant, who'd unfolded the fabric. Then it killed the tailor's stepson and four neighbours. Soon the devastating disease gripped the whole of Eyam. The cures hadn't worked. When a victim coughed blood and came out in large boils, live chickens or *toads were strapped to the swellings so that, when they burst, the animal absorbed the poisons. Yet the treatment hadn't slowed the disease. And neither had medicinal drinks made from herbs and human body wastes.*

To make sure that the plague did not spread to Matlock, Sheffield, Bakewell, Buxton and beyond, the brave people of Eyam had quarantined themselves from the rest of England. Emmott was forced to cut herself off from Rowland, while a third of her village died.

At least Rowland and Emmott could see each other from afar. But then in spring, Emmott failed to show. Rowland would not give up on her, though. His longing for Emmott was too strong for that. He returned faithfully to the same spot every single day until December, even though Emmott never again appeared at the arch.

Close to Christmas, Eyam was declared free of the terrible disease and Rowland was the first to enter the shattered village. Breathless, he ran straight to Emmott's home but found it empty. Emmott had died back in April, along with most of her family. She hadn't even had a proper burial. Eyam's churchyard had not been able to cope with the sudden demand for graves so, like most of the other victims, Emmott had been laid to rest in her garden, without a funeral.

And worst of all, Rowland had not been there to say goodbye. He had not been there to hold her while she passed away.

Broken hearted and angry, Rowland scratched a message of eternal love on a piece of lead and threw it into the village well. Then he crossed the village and sat, head bowed, in the stone arch where the beautiful young woman who was to be his wife had once stood, gazing down at him from afar.

1

For a few seconds, Seth thought that the tour guide must have mistaken them for a load of primary school kids, because she was chanting an old nursery rhyme. Perhaps it was an April Fools' joke.

"*Ring-a-ring o' roses, A pocket full of posies. A-tishoo! A-tishoo! We all fall down.*" Yet it was a wicked smile that came to her face. "It might sound jolly, but it's very cruel really, because it's about the Black Death here in Eyam in the seventeenth century. The 'ring o' roses' was the horrible red rash on the victims' bodies. The 'posies' were the herbs that didn't cure it, and 'a-tishoo' was the sneezing that spread it around. It was the plague that made everyone 'fall down' – dead."

The trip to Eyam was the first of two school visits near the end of the spring term. Seth's group had come to a halt just off a lane that led sharply downhill into the Derbyshire village. They had formed a semicircle around a dreary monument, covered in moss and algae.

Just as the school party was getting bored with the chat about a nursery rhyme, the local guide began to talk in gruesome detail about the symptoms of the Black Death: vomiting, coughing blood, unstoppable diarrhoea, dark blotches in the neck, armpits and groin, and the suffocating stench of death.

Deciding that the disease was no joke, Seth

screwed up his face in disgust. The plague may have been three hundred and forty years ago, but the thought of unending diarrhoea and bleeding in the groin grabbed everyone's attention. When the guide told them how people would moan, groan and scream as they came out in unbearably painful black boils, filled with blood and pus, half of the students grimaced. The other half looked at each other and grinned. But Wes Radcliffe was not one for wincing. Unable to keep a straight face, he nudged Seth's twin sister, Kim, and said, "What a bloody mess."

Kim smiled back, then pulled her best vampire face and said, "Dripping gore. Yummy."

Standing next to them at the end of the line of pupils, Seth was much more subdued.

The tour guide continued, "The village vicars, William Mompesson and Thomas Stanley, persuaded the villagers to make a superhuman sacrifice. Even knowing that many of them would die, they promised to stay put and cut themselves off from the rest of the country so they didn't spread the disease. People living in the surrounding area left food and supplies for them either at the southern edge of the village, or right here. The survivors had to pay for everything, but their coins were contaminated, so they put them in this well where the running water would wash away the seeds of plague." The tour guide pointed down at the spring that was partly covered by a grubby, concrete hood. "It became known later as Mompesson's Well."

She turned slightly towards the south and said, "There wasn't any running water at the other drop-off point so they cut holes in a boulder called the Boundary Stone and left silver shillings in the hollows, covered with vinegar to clean them of the sickness."

Wes peered into the discoloured water of Mompesson's Well and muttered sarcastically, "Exciting."

Kim elbowed him and whispered, "Look, there's money in it."

"Is there?" Wes glanced down again and nodded. There were at least three pound coins, a couple of fifty-pence pieces and some other coins that Wes didn't recognize. "Yeah. Real money."

When the school party began to snake away from the monument, the guide and a teacher at its head, Wes lingered and knelt down at the edge of the well.

"I don't think you ought to..." Seth said to his mate. But he was too late.

Wes's hand was already in the slimy water, scooping out a handful of cold coins.

"Wesley!" Mr. Hanif yelled. "What are you doing?"

"Nothing, sir," Wes replied. Quickly, he closed his fist around the icy loot. "Just tying my shoelaces."

"Well, hurry up."

"That's a good one, sir. Well! Geddit?" Wes grinned and nodded towards the well before straightening up.

"Come on! Seth and Kim as well."

Kim laughed. "Well, well. Another well," she said, trying to distract the history teacher from Wes.

Behind Seth, Wes slipped the cash into his pocket and wiped his wet hand on his trousers. He could feel the coins against his leg. They were surprisingly heavy and, even through the material, they felt uncannily cold against his skin, making him shudder.

It wasn't a fantastic haul. Wes, Kim and Seth got nearly a pound each. But they stood a chance of getting more. After they'd shared out the modern money, they were left with one unrecognizable, dull rectangle about the size of a domino and three diamond-shaped silvery coins carrying a date of 1646. Kim and Wes would have thrown them away as useless, but Seth stopped them. He poked the coins with his forefinger, but couldn't bring himself to pick them up. "Look, they're more than three hundred years old," he said. "Could be worth a lot."

"And what are we going to do about it?" Kim replied.

"It's Saturday tomorrow," Seth said to his sister. "We'll get the tram into town. Don't you remember that shop near Castle Market that bought Nan's old junk when she died?"

Wes looked at Kim and shrugged. "Worth a try, I guess."

Kim agreed. "It's my tournament on Sunday and I want to put some practice in but I've got time, I suppose."

Twins were supposed to have an uncanny and unspoken understanding. But Seth didn't share a subconscious, almost mystical link with Kim. At times, he barely shared a conscious one with her. He stuck with her, though, because she was his sister and she'd become a firm friend of his best mate. Perhaps Wes and Kim had hit it off because they could be as bad as each other. They were often in trouble and seemed to egg each other on.

There was another reason. Whenever things went wrong for Kim, Mum and Dad always put part of the blame on Seth. "A brother should look out for his sister," they would mutter. "Especially because you're older – by thirteen minutes." This was meant as a joke, he knew, but then they'd add, "Besides, you're the sensible one. You should've stopped her." As if he – or anyone else – could control Kim. His parents didn't know that Kim made it impossible for him to keep an eye on her. But she was still his twin, after all, and sometimes he admired her wildly adventurous spirit.

Today was no different. Something inside Seth told him that the stolen coins were trouble. He had seen how Wes's whole body shivered when he put them into his trouser pocket. Seth felt uneasy, but he couldn't help going along with his sister and friend.

2

In Sheffield city centre, the shabby shop window was a mass of museum pieces that their grandparents and great grandparents would have recognized. Medals, an album of postage stamps, models of steam trains and bygone aeroplanes, tatty teddy bears, coins, all sorts of trinkets. When Wes, Seth and Kim went inside Hancock's Collectables, it was like walking back through time. It even smelled old.

The man behind the counter was not as ancient as they'd expected, and nowhere near as old as the stuff that he sold. His eyebrows rose when he saw the three teenagers. "What can I do for you?" he said.

Wes held out the coins on his palm. "We've got these."

"Oh?" The dealer looked at the silvery diamonds and laughed. "Somebody's been to Eyam!"

"What do you mean?" Seth asked.

"They're imitations of silver shillings. They're made for visitors – sold for a few pence. Tourists buy them and then throw them in the well. I don't know why. For luck, maybe, or out of respect for what the village did." For an instant he looked surprised. "If you've been there, you should know. Didn't you buy them in the museum's shop?"

"We went to Eyam," Seth answered. "But it was a school trip. We didn't get to buy anything."

Wes cut into the conversation. "Are you saying they're not worth much?"

The man shook his head. "Let me have a closer look – just in case." When Wes tipped the coins onto the dealer's palm, the man frowned. Right away, he set aside two fakes, but he took a lot more interest in the other two pieces. He weighed the third shilling in his hand, mumbled something about how heavy it was, and examined it through a magnifying glass. Looking stunned, he said to the youngsters, "You know, this is the real thing. Amazing, to say the least."

"What's it worth?" asked Kim, more interested in cash than surprises.

"Did it come from Eyam?"

"Yeah. We found it on the ground – like the others," Kim fibbed.

"Quite a find." The shopkeeper smiled and shook his head at their astonishing piece of luck.

"What's it worth?" Kim repeated.

"That depends. In this condition – very good – it'd fetch somewhere between five hundred and seven hundred pounds. That's what a collector would pay. If you're asking what I'd give you for it: four hundred."

For a while, they didn't know what to say. They just gaped at each other. Then Seth muttered, "Four hundred pounds!"

"You'd better think what you want to do while I..." The shopkeeper tapped the final grubby relic, to show that he wanted to take a closer look. When he turned it over, he shivered. Looking puzzled, he peered at it through the thick lens.

Wes went into a huddle with the twins. "Brilliant!" he said.

"We could auction it on eBay," Kim replied, "and get more. Like seven hundred."

"Yeah, but we might not," Seth warned his sister. "And we'd have to wait for at least a couple of weeks before we get the dosh."

"It'd be a cheque. What could we do with a cheque?" Wes shrugged.

"It's up to you," Seth whispered to Wes. "You fished it out."

"I'll take the money," said Wes.

Kim was about to argue when the antique dealer interrupted.

"This is valuable. Not in terms of money, you understand. I mean, historically valuable." He held the grey rectangle in both hands, a bridge between his fingers. "It's a piece of lead with a message written on it. It's heavy and it bends, see? Back then, there was a lot of lead mining thereabouts. Eyam Museum's where this belongs."

"A message?" Seth prompted.

"Yes. It's hard to decipher," the shopkeeper replied. "It's very old – and worn. I think it's for someone called Emma. It'll be a simple message. You've got to remember, if it's from the seventeenth century, a lot of folk couldn't write." Looking up at them with a grin, he added, "No e-mails or text messages then." Using the magnifying glass again, he said hesitantly, "It needs an expert really, but I think it's *Emma, true love always, rest in peace, R.T.*"

Wes wasn't interested in a love message, so he changed the subject. "We'll have the four hundred."

Behind the counter, the man took a deep breath. He was probably disappointed that his young customers weren't taking an interest in history. "Okay. But I don't keep that sort of money in the shop. Have you got a bank account?"

All three of them shook their heads.

"Okay. So you can't use a cheque. You'll have to come back after lunch – when I've had a chance to go to the bank. I'll give you the money in cash if you promise me one thing."

Kim frowned. "What's that?"

The shopkeeper gave her the piece of lead. "It doesn't feel right, does it? Sort of cold." He wiped his fingers on his jumper.

Kim weighed it in her hand and turned up her nose. Quickly, she passed it back to Wes.

"Anyway," the man said, "promise me you'll take it back to Eyam. It's important."

"Is it?" Wes asked.

He nodded. "It says *Rest in peace.* You've got to respect that. Put it back where you got it or give it to the museum." He paused, apparently deciding whether to tell them something else. He cleared his throat and then added, "You know, one of the most tragic figures at Eyam was a Mrs. Hancock. She buried her husband and six children. Her entire family gone in one week – apart from one son, who lived and worked here in Sheffield."

"So?"

"I'm John Hancock, descended from her only surviving son." He pointed at the lead tablet and said, "So, I know how much something like this means to the village, even after all these years. Mark my words. Take it back."

3

Staring at the wad of twenty-pound notes that Wes was holding, Kim beamed. It was the most money that she'd ever seen in one bundle. "How do we split it?" she asked, eagerly.

Wes looked surprised. "Who says we're going to split it?"

"Because...because we're mates," Kim replied.

"And who told you there was money in the well anyway?"

Wes laughed. "I had you there. Course we'll share it. But three into four hundred doesn't go."

"I spotted the shilling in the first place," Kim said, "and you grabbed it. I don't know what Seth did."

Seth gave his twin a withering look. "I thought of going to the shop."

"Oh, dangerous," Kim muttered sarcastically.

Wes intervened. "You two always get the same. Birthday, Christmas, your mum and dad always make sure your presents are worth the same. And spotting coins in a well wasn't exactly dangerous, either, Kim. I took all the risks."

"Huh."

"Look," Wes said. "I'll have two hundred and you two have a hundred each. Yeah?"

The twins started talking at the same time. While Seth said, "All right," Kim complained, "That's not fair..."

"It's a hundred pounds more than you would've got if Wes kept it all," Seth pointed out. "Or if he hadn't nicked it in the first place."

"It's not nicking," Wes protested. "If you take money out of people's pockets, that's nicking. I just took stuff they'd left lying around, like picking up an apple that's fallen off someone else's tree."

Kim pounced straight away. "If it's not thieving, you didn't take any risks."

Wes smiled. "What if Mr. Hanif had seen me? Course there was a risk."

Seth sighed. "This isn't getting us anywhere. Let's just carve it up the way you said."

With five of the twenty-pound notes in her hand, Kim felt better. Money always had that effect on her. When she was eleven, she used to go round the tennis courts challenging older boys to a game at one pound a time. They always accepted, because it looked like easy money, because they thought that a girl barely bigger than her racket couldn't possibly beat them, and because it didn't do their masculinity any good to refuse. Kim would lose the occasional game but, over a full session on court, she always walked away with a grin and a profit. Those exploits made her confident and comfortable among boys and her cheek won the admiration of girls. Right now, she wanted the cash for a new coat and a state-of-the-art tennis racket.

Seth asked, "How are we going to get back to Eyam?"

"Back to Eyam? What for?"

"To take that lump of lead back. We promised."

Wes shrugged. "We didn't. Forget it. It doesn't matter, just a stupid message." He reached into his pocket, touched the ice-cold metal, and withdrew his hand at once.

Kim agreed. "It's not like Emma or R.T. are around to thank us."

"They might be angry we took it in the first place," said Seth. "They won't be best pleased if we don't take it back."

Wes and Kim laughed aloud.

"Don't be daft," Kim cried. "They're dead! It's not like they can come and get us."

"Skeletons don't have the equipment to be angry or pleased," Wes added with a grin.

Unconvinced, Seth turned away.

Lined up at the bottom of the central escalator in Meadowhall Shopping Centre, the three friends peered into the trickling water feature. "What do you think, then?" Wes asked Kim.

Kim shifted the bulging plastic bag that held the coat and tennis racket she'd just bought. She leaned over the rail, trying to identify and count the coins that seemed to jostle around under the rippling surface of the pool. "I don't know. Hard to see, but there's got to be twenty quid in there. Maybe more."

Wes nodded. "Rich pickings."

"If you ask me—" Seth began.

"We didn't," Kim said at once, cutting him short with a smile.

"Well, I reckon it's a no-go," Seth continued. "There's a million and one people watching."

"It's not nicking, remember," Wes replied. "If people are daft enough to throw their money away – and leave it lying here – they can't blame us for helping ourselves."

"Yeah," Kim agreed. "Why do people chuck perfectly good money in a fountain, anyway?"

"It's supposed to bring good luck, isn't it?" Wes answered. Then, with a grin, he added, "It'll bring *us* good luck."

Seth shook his head. He was worried that their stroke of luck with the Eyam coin had made Kim and Wes into total money addicts. It wouldn't take much to turn Kim into a complete shopaholic. Whenever she wasn't hanging out with Wes or her tennis mates, she seemed to be shopping with her girlfriends. More than that, she seemed to be competing with them to wear the best designer clothes.

Seth read from the notice at the end of the feature. "*The proceeds from this water feature will be donated to the Northern General Hospital.* That's why they throw cash in here. If you...you know... it'd be like robbing the hospital."

"It doesn't belong to the hospital yet," Wes replied.

Kim nodded. "Don't be so boring, Seth. It's just sitting here getting wet, and no one's going to get hurt."

A little boy ran up to the barricade and tossed a ten-pence piece into the water. Then he closed his eyes and screwed up his face for a few seconds, probably making a wish. Afterwards, looking pleased with himself, he toddled back to his parents.

Once the boy was out of hearing, Seth said, "Even if it was a good idea, how would you nick the money with so many people watching?"

Kim sighed. "We don't do it now. We've got day

tickets for the tram. We come back after I've put a bit of practice in." She mimicked a backhand passing shot. "When does the place close? Eight o'clock. So, we do it at two minutes to eight, when the place is more-or-less empty."

"Spot on," Wes said. "With hoods up, so the security cameras don't catch us. We grab the cash and run like hell. Easy. Are you in on it?"

Seth thought about it for a moment. He'd got a hundred pounds in his pocket. That was a lot already. It was a major boost to his meagre savings towards his own computer. But he was still a long way short. Besides, he didn't really want to miss out on their scam, even though he felt ill at ease. And he was supposed to be looking after his sister, keeping her out of trouble. "Yeah. All right. I'll come. But—"

"No buts," Kim said. "You come or you don't. That's it."

"Count me in, then." But Seth had a bad feeling about it.

4

Back at home, Seth hid his money in his bedroom, with his other savings, before he went down for tea. Over the meal, Kim told their mum and dad that she'd got a really cheap coat and a fantastic tennis racket in the sales. That way, she didn't have to explain how she'd come up with such a lot of cash. Then, after tea, she went outside to rehearse a few shots with her new racket, ready to use it in the tennis tournament tomorrow.

She'd also booked a session on the indoor court for the evening. But before that, she had something else to do.

In the shopping centre, they waited until closing time when the place was almost deserted. Checking that no one was nearby, Kim and Wes vaulted over the handrail, just as they'd planned, and splashed into the water. It came up to their knees and it was so chilly that it made them shiver. Seth leaned over the barrier and held out an open plastic bag. Wes was the first to scoop coins into his cupped hands and dump them hurriedly into the bag. The weight of the cash tightened the plastic handles on Seth's fingers and water dripped out of the small holes at the bottom of the bag. Seconds later, Kim added some more. When Wes plonked a second, smaller batch of coins into the bag, it felt promisingly heavy.

Seth kept his hood up and his head down. "That's enough," he whispered. The cash left in the pool was more spread out and would take too long to gather together.

"One more," Kim replied breathlessly, but with a smile. Plainly, she was enjoying herself. In her mind, she was probably spending the money already.

Seth hated every second. He glanced around and, out of the corner of his eye, caught sight of a girl on crutches. She was standing unnaturally still outside a music shop, watching them from a distance. She was leaning crookedly to one side, and she looked as if she belonged to a different age. Her clothes were anything but stylish and her long mousy hair was unkempt. There was an expression of disgust on her face.

"Quickly!" Seth whispered. "Someone's watching us."

Kim fished out the last handful of coins and dropped them into the plastic bag. She clambered out of the water and leaped athletically over the barrier.

"Let's go!" said Wes, as he followed her.

The old-fashioned girl just stood there silently watching them, swaying like a rickety signpost in the wind.

Seth was already feeling guilty about his part in the stunt before the mystery girl appeared. Now, he felt even worse, but at least she couldn't chase them.

They took off along The Arcade towards the exit nearest to the tram station. As Wes and Kim ran, their sopping wet trainers made exaggerated slapping noises on the floor, leaving little puddles on the glossy tiles.

Just as the three of them reached the exit, a man's angry voice sounded somewhere behind them. "Oi! You!" They didn't hesitate or turn round. They escaped from the mall as quickly as they could and made a dash for the bridge to Meadowhall

Interchange. Drips continued to fly from Kim's and Wes's jeans and trainers, but they weren't leaving wet footprints any more. The cash clunked in the plastic bag as Seth sprinted.

A tram was waiting at the terminus, its welcoming doors open. Breathing heavily, the three friends dived inside and plonked themselves down. "Phew! Lucky," Wes said with an excited smile.

Kim bent down and pulled her sodden trousers away from her legs. "Yuck. That's horrible."

"Yeah," Wes agreed, "but we made it. Fantastic."

Kim nodded and laughed.

Seth looked anxiously at the open doors and said to himself, "I wish it'd get going."

"Relax." Wes reached out for the carrier bag. "You didn't drop any, did you? Let's see what we got."

Seth was glad to give up their pickings. He felt less shame when the hospital's cash wasn't in his hands. While Wes and Kim peered into the bag with grins on their faces, Seth kept watch on the entrance to the tram station. He jumped when he saw two security guards race into the Interchange, grind to a halt, and look around.

5

Seth shrank in his seat, his heart thudding in his chest. Guessing that the men were the ones who had shouted at them in the mall, Seth whispered, "There!" He nodded towards the window and the two beefy men outside.

All three of them ducked down.

When a couple of elderly passengers further along

the stationary coach peered at them suspiciously, Wes put his hand into the carrier bag, grabbed a couple of coins and dropped them as if by accident. Then he said loudly, "Oops. Where've they gone?"

It gave Kim, Seth and Wes an excuse to get down and scrabble on the floor, out of sight of the men.

One of the other passengers made a tutting noise and muttered, "Teenagers!"

After a minute of pretend-searching, Kim dared to pop up and glance out of the window. With a gulp, she saw that one security officer was walking along the platform, glancing into the tram as he went. The other was heading for the railway station. She bent down again and said quietly, "One of them's coming."

"Do you want to make a run for it?" asked Wes.

Kim shook her head. "He'll see us, and the other one's lurking over by the trains."

Seth said nothing. He just cowered, feigning a search for the money, and wished that he'd managed to persuade them not to steal the coins in the first place.

The security man's face appeared at the furthest window of their coach. Within seconds, he'd be close enough to spot them.

Seth held his breath.

But, just as they were about to be discovered, the doors closed with a hiss and the tram eased its way out of the terminus.

Seth sighed heavily and the other two cheered. When some passengers scowled at them, Wes said aloud, "It's all right. Found our money." He held up a pound coin for everyone to see as he got back into his seat.

The tram picked up speed, made a wide sweep round the shopping complex and headed for the city centre. Kim looked at her watch and grinned. "If I don't hang about, I'll even be on time for my slot on the indoor court."

Kim didn't want to take a load of cash to the

sports club. She agreed that Wes should keep the money and they'd share it out later, when tennis wasn't top of her list of priorities.

On Sunday, Kim was off form. Her arms and legs had begun to ache as if she was starting a nasty cold. She was one of the favourites for the tennis trophy, so she expected to trounce her rivals, but her serve wasn't working, her movement around the court was sluggish, her spin was predictable and the ball strayed outside the line or into the net far too often. Her play didn't even improve when she abandoned her new racket and used her trusty old one instead.

Kim's opponents were surprised and clearly delighted to see a top seed knocked out so early in the competition.

* * *

"Romans!" Kim muttered scornfully to her girlfriends as their coach zoomed up the motorway towards York on Monday. It was the second Year-8 trip of the spring term and the group was going to study the effect of Romans on the development of Britain. Kim was still annoyed about her performance in the tennis tournament the previous day, and her cold was making her miserable. "They wore togas, built straight roads, and had a real good time killing Brits and boozing. What else is there to know?"

Overhearing her, Mr. Hanif replied, "Plenty. They gave us the modern calendar, numerals, villas, baths and lots more besides. You'll see."

In Museum Gardens, the students couldn't see much at all. It was foggy. The museum itself, a few trees, and the ruins of St. Leonard's Hospital and a fortress loomed out of the grey mist. Squirrels ran around freely on the grass, pigeons scrounged crusts and crisps, and a Roman soldier stood in front of the school group.

"Welcome to Eboracum," the soldier announced. He was dressed ridiculously as a legionnaire, complete with body armour, spear and shield. "You're standing on it right now. If you dig down just a foot or so anywhere around here, you'll find Roman remains." He paused and added in a quivery voice, "Quite possibly skeletons."

Straight away, Kim put her hand up. "Do you dig coins up?"

"Certainly," the soldier-cum-guide answered. "A few skeletons found around here had coins inside their skulls. You see, some Romans thought the dead had to pay Charon – the ferryman – to take them across the river Styx into the underworld. So, they put a coin in the mouth of a dead relative so he or she could pay the ferryman.

"Anyway," he said, "I'm getting ahead of myself. I'm going to show you how Romans bathed, exercised, fought, died, and went to the toilet. And you're going to complete a quiz sheet. First, we're going to go down to the bathhouse, where they didn't use soap. They got clean by sweating the dirt out of their skin and then scraping it off with a piece of metal. If you're really lucky, you'll get to see a Roman sewer. Then it's back here for lunch in the grounds and a look around the museum. We'll finish in the cellar of the Treasurer's House, where there's an excavated bit of cobbled Roman road, notable for being haunted. A plumber working down there saw a whole legion of Roman soldiers walking right through the cellar wall, along the route of the original road, to the sound of a trumpet. So, keep your eyes peeled and your ears pinned back! You never know what you might see or hear. Now, onward, troops!"

As the kids groaned and trudged away, the bells of York Minster rang ominously.

When the school group returned to Museum Gardens, the place was eerily quiet. There was no wind and mist hung in the still air, muffling the sound of the modern city beyond the gates. Some of the students sat in the ruins of St. Leonard's Hospital eating their packed lunches. It was damp and spooky among the shabby pillars and arches, making it easy to imagine the thirteenth-century patients suffering primitive treatments and dying in dreadful pain under the low ceiling.

Other pupils had gone off into the garden to feed or frighten the legions of pigeons.

Kim abandoned her girlfriends in favour of Wes and her brother. Seth thought he knew why. He believed that their good fortune with the coins had bound the three of them together. Now, he felt they were more than a gang. Not quite thieves, but bandits perhaps. To Seth, a bandit sounded nicer than a thief.

They wandered over to part of the ruins called the Multangular Tower. Once, it had formed the western corner of an impressive Roman fortress. Now, less than half of it remained. Standing at its base, among six stone coffins arranged in a semicircle, the three friends looked up. The broken tower still seemed high. It wrapped itself around them and, together with the fog, it cut them off from the rest of the party.

Five of the coffins were open and contained a layer of silt. The sixth had a stone lid, but it was askew as if a shrunken hand had reached up from inside and pushed it open to the living world. One of the other coffins was smaller and sadder than the rest. It must have been made for a child.

When Seth breathed out, the mist swirled in front of him. Movement on the ground caught his eye and made him jump. Yet it was only a squirrel. It came out from behind the last coffin, walked cheekily past Wes, and began to scrabble in the damp earth in front of the partly closed coffin. It wasn't even put off when Wes blew his nose.

"Must be used to people," Kim said, taking a step towards it and throwing a crisp in its direction.

The creature ignored the titbit and carried on digging, its bushy tail poking up.

"I don't think squirrels are into prawn cocktail flavour," Seth replied. "It's buried a nut or something."

Kim gazed at the animal for a while and then continued to tiptoe towards it. "What's the odds I can catch it?" she whispered.

Wes sniffed and then laughed. "Nil."

"You're on," Kim muttered, glancing back at Wes with a grin. "Watch this."

Fog lingered over the opening in the tomb, making Seth wonder what remained inside. For a few seconds, his whole body quivered. Then, distracted by his sister, he turned towards the unsuspecting squirrel.

Slowly, Kim took one more step and began to lean forwards and down, her arms out, ready to lunge at the creature.

Seth knew she was fooling around. She didn't

really expect to catch it. She would have been horrified if she had, and let the poor thing go straight away. His twin wasn't cruel.

Wes let out a huge cough. At the sound, the squirrel darted away, its grey tail bobbing behind it.

"Cheat!" Kim cried, laughing and stopping herself from toppling over by grabbing the lip of the stone coffin.

Wes tried to look offended. "Huh. You're not the only one bunged up with a cold, you know. My throat's killing me."

Kim turned towards Wes and Seth, but her eyes focused on something behind them. "Hey," she called. "What are you doing?"

Seth spun round. Two boys from the same school were huddled over a small exhibit box on a pole. One of them used a stone to smash the small padlock that held down the lid.

Kim steamed towards them. "That's not very nice, is it?" she said, pretending to be shocked. "Vandals."

"There's something inside," the boy said, letting go of the stone. "Could be valuable."

Joining Kim, Wes said, "Course there's something inside. It's an exhibition."

When Seth came up as well, it was three against two, and the boys retreated, mumbling as they went.

The top of the box was made of thick plastic and behind it was a piece of dull metal. The inscription plate had been covered with graffiti, so they couldn't read it, but they recognized that the relic was another piece of lead.

Taking advantage of the broken lock, Kim lifted the lid and slipped her hand inside. Her fingers closed around the metal tablet, slightly wider than her palm. As she pulled it out, she joked, "Shame to just leave it here. Someone might swipe it." Then she added, "And those boys might be right. You never know what it's worth." But from the look on Seth's face, she could see he didn't approve.

6

The teachers had called the school group back together by the fortress wall where the mock legionnaire was delivering another lecture. "Romans brought a bit of class to Britain, you know. Ancient Britons threw their dead bodies out with the rubbish, but Romans were more refined. They buried their dead – along with their prized possessions – or cremated them and kept their ashes in lead pots. When important rich people died, they put them in these stone coffins." He waved his spear towards the foot of the Multangular Tower, where Kim had snaffled her treasure. Luckily, from where he stood, the guide couldn't see that the exhibit box had been vandalized. "They put the coffins in carved tombs and left them on show above ground."

Kim was standing at the back of the pack, masked by the fog, examining the relic in her palm. Having seen R.T.'s message to the girl called Emma, Kim recognized the object as a piece of lead with writing scratched onto it. But this time, she didn't stand a chance of reading the inscription, because it was in Latin. She placed it inside her rucksack, with her emptied sandwich box.

"Mind you, Romans and Brits could both be horrid," the ancient soldier was saying. "Early Britons – Celts and Druids – threw severed human heads into the river or a nearby lake as gifts to the gods. Romans appeased the spirits of the evil dead with all sorts of gruesome offerings."

Wes piped up, "Did Romans write things on lead?"

The guide smiled broadly. "Very perceptive. Yes, they did, young man. You can see examples in the museum and – if you get the time – look at the exhibit down by the stone coffins. If you were Roman, you could curse someone who'd wronged you by writing a complaint to the gods on lead and chucking it into a spring or river. The curses were much nastier than today's community service or anti-social behaviour orders. 'May you be buried alive or eaten slowly by wild dogs.' That sort of thing. The ones to watch, though, were written backwards. That was supposed to make the magic stronger. They turn up occasionally when the Ouse floods, or in a dried-up well." The soldier lifted up his shield and said in a loud voice, "Now, to the museum, troops."

* * *

Back at home after the school trip, the three friends huddled together on the fallen log in the rough ground behind Wes's house at the edge of Sheffield. In front of them was a small, messy pond and beyond the water was a run-down farm. A cow was brushing up against the flimsy fence, apparently using the wire to scratch an itch.

Kim didn't notice. She was paying more attention to the piece of lead she'd stumbled across in York. With her finger, she followed the worn words etched onto its surface.

"What's it say?" Seth asked.

"How do I know?" Kim replied, wrapped in her brand-new coat. She sneezed loudly twice.

Seth could tell that his sister was off colour. "It's probably Latin. We could show it to a teacher," he said. "Mr. Hanif might know that sort of thing."

"No," Kim replied. "That'd be like Hancock's Collectables all over again. We'd get in big trouble and he'd make us take it back."

"We haven't taken the Eyam one back," Seth pointed out miserably, his scruples coming to the surface again.

"That was horrible to touch and it really hurt when it rubbed against me," Wes complained. "Made me feel terrible, so I chucked it." He broke off a fungus from the decaying log and threw it into the shallow pond.

Seth watched him and said, "Yuck. That's probably poisonous or something."

"Don't be daft!"

"You shouldn't have ditched R.T.'s message," Seth muttered. "It was important. We should've taken it back."

"We've got more important things to do with our time," Wes replied.

"Yeah. Like share out the Meadowhall loot," said Kim.

Wes looked over his shoulder at his house. "Not now, eh?"

The fog had gone. Only a thin mist remained eerily above the stagnant water. But it was beginning to get dark. The cow ambled away from the wire fence, leaving it seriously bowed.

"Have you got it safe?" Kim asked.

"Er... Now that you mention it...where did I...?"

"Stop mucking about."

"Yeah. I've got it. Somewhere." Wes laughed and cleared his throat at the same time. "It's under my bed."

"When are we going to share it out?" Kim nagged.

"When we're not on a school trip, you're not playing tennis and my mum isn't around." Changing the subject, he touched the Roman relic in Kim's hand. "This one's different. Not like R.T.'s. It's not cold for one thing. I'll tell you what. We could trace the writing onto paper and show Hanif that."

Kim nodded and smiled. "Hey, you're not as dumb as you look. But what happens when he asks where we got it?"

Wes shrugged. "We saw it in the museum and traced it, because we thought it'd look good in our project. But we didn't want to put it in without knowing what it says. Anyway, it might be really gory. Excellent."

Seth nodded his agreement.

"Sounds okay to me," Kim said. Then she succumbed to a fit of coughing.

Before they moved on, they did what they'd always done. Seth and Kim bent down and picked up a stone each. Wes grabbed two. "Ready?" he asked. Underarm, he tossed his first stone high into the air. It plopped into the pond near the centre and created a circular ripple. They all took careful aim as he counted, "One, two, three, go!"

The ritual required them to throw their stones within the expanding ring. Anyone who waited till it was easy, or missed the target would be mocked. If any of the stones hit each other in mid-air, it was cause for a special celebration. And they usually shared a good argument about whose stone was closest to the middle.

This time, Kim and Wes hit dead centre and slapped each other's hands. Seth's stone landed apart from the other two, but just within the circle. He narrowly avoided a thorough teasing.

At the end of school on Tuesday, Mr. Hanif looked closely at the piece of tracing paper. "Mmm. It's not very clear. I suppose that's not surprising after a couple of thousand years – and after being traced. It's a pity I can't examine the real thing."

"But can you translate it?" asked Kim.

"I should be able to, but it doesn't... Hang on. It's like the guide said. It's Latin all right, but it's backwards. That means it's a grim curse. Let's see." He squinted at the scribble and transcribed it onto another scrap of paper. "It's along the lines of, *He who wears another's cloak will be crushed to a rotting corpse.*" He looked up at them with a grin. "Charming. Obviously written by someone who's miffed about having his cloak stolen."

"How would anyone be crushed?" Seth asked, grimacing.

"I don't know," Mr. Hanif answered. "Maybe under a falling stone."

"How about a traffic accident?" Wes joked. "Run over by a chariot."

"That's not as crazy as it sounds," Mr. Hanif replied.

Kim laughed and said, "Thanks."

"No problem. I'm surprised and delighted by the effort you're putting in." The history teacher smiled. "Makes me look forward to reading your project."

When they turned to go, Kim crashed clumsily into a chair. Somehow, she got tangled in its legs and tripped. As she fell, she put out her right arm to break her fall. Her hand slammed down at an awkward angle and let out a grotesque crack. At the same time, she screamed with shock and pain.

Seth gasped. For some reason, the Eyam nursery rhyme came into his head. *Ring-a-ring o' roses, A pocket full of posies. A-tishoo! A-tishoo! We all fall down.*

Mr. Hanif kneeled at Kim's side, looking very concerned. He held out a hand. "Let me see it."

Still sprawled on the classroom floor, Kim nursed her right arm in her left hand. Her face was contorted with agony, and tears had come involuntarily to her eyes. Disbelief was plain in her expression – but so was the knowledge that something awful had happened. Meekly, she held out her arm.

"Can you move your wrist?" Mr. Hanif asked softly.

"No."

The teacher nodded. "Okay. I think you might've broken it."

Looking devastated, she muttered, "But it's my tennis hand."

7

The school nurse put a support on Kim's wrist and then Mr. Hanif drove her to the Accident and Emergency Unit of the Northern General Hospital. The teacher registered Kim at the reception and told Seth to phone his parents.

Not getting an answer from either, Seth left a message on his mum's mobile.

The teacher sighed. "Never mind. The school nurse'll call your mum and dad as well – that's the procedure." He hesitated before adding, "The trouble is, I've got to go and pick my daughter up from her school. Sorry, but Kim's in good hands here and your mum or dad'll get the message soon enough. After I've got my daughter, I'll call the hospital and check your parents have turned up. Okay?"

Seth shrugged. "Sure. Thanks."

Mr. Hanif left the three friends safely in the waiting area.

The place was seething with all sorts of disasters. A baby was screaming as its mother paced frantically up and down. A man in a rugby kit was nursing a damaged shoulder. Several people were sitting quietly, staring into space. A woman just along the bench was in a neck brace that looked like scaffolding around her head. She remained as rigid as a stone statue.

Seth looked at his sister and thought about the Roman curse that was in the pocket of her new coat right now. *He who wears another's cloak will be crushed to a rotting corpse.* He wondered if her coat counted as a stolen cloak. Kim had bought it with the money they'd got from raiding Mompesson's Well. Because the cash wasn't theirs, the coat shouldn't really belong to her.

Seth leaned towards her and said in a low voice, "The York curse is a lot more serious than Eyam's rest-in-peace and love message."

At once, Kim exploded. "How can you think about that when I'm like this?"

"But—"

"I won't be able to play tennis!"

"It's just that –" Seth decided that it was pointless to try and explain. "Nothing."

"What?" she demanded to know.

"I was just thinking, maybe your hand and the curse... Oh, it doesn't matter."

"You're crazy."

Whenever the twins were at each other's throats or slinging insults back and forth, Seth could almost convince himself that he wouldn't care if Kim were crushed to a rotting corpse. He did care, really. It was just the sort of thing people living too close together felt when tempers flared. The thought that the spell might be coming true tormented him. He didn't try to tell Kim and Wes, though, because they wouldn't believe him. Worse, they'd make fun of the idea. Besides, Kim's wrist wasn't crushed exactly.

He glanced at his mobile and wondered if his mum had got his message yet. There was no sign of her.

Waiting for what seemed to be an eternity in a torture chamber, Seth was ashamed that they'd wronged the hospital by stealing the charity money. If the staff knew, they'd keep Kim hanging around in pain for even longer. He watched a patient with an extreme limp being taken away for treatment, certain that he'd arrived after Kim. Seth glanced at his sister again. She seemed pale and tired. Both Kim and Wes had closed their eyes and appeared to be dozing. Even in a light sleep, pain was written across his twin's troubled face.

Quietly, Seth got to his feet and padded back to the reception desk. Pausing for a trolley to come past him, he looked down a long, wide corridor on his right, leading into the heart of the hospital. At first, the sight of a girl on crutches hobbling away from him did not strike him as unusual but, when she turned into one of the side rooms, he caught his breath. It was the same girl who had watched them snatching the money from Meadowhall Shopping Centre. It was all over in a second. The door closed on the frail figure and she'd gone.

Shaken, Seth went up to the desk and waited his turn. "It's my sister," he said nervously. "She's been waiting ages."

"We're dealing with everyone as quickly as we can," the harassed receptionist replied.

"But people coming in after her have been seen."

She sighed. "Give me her name."

"Kim Treanor." He spelled the surname, just to make sure.

The receptionist checked her monitor and then, looking puzzled, rummaged through the papers littering the desk. "Did you report in when you arrived?"

"Yes," Seth answered. "My teacher did."

"Well, I'm sorry, but we've got no record of her. That's why she's not been seen. Give me her address and age, and tell me what's happened to her. I'll see what I can do to speed her up."

Afterwards, Seth nipped outside to phone his mum again, hoping that she'd arrive like a cavalry and put everything right. This time, she replied in person and denied that her phone had recorded any messages. Instead, she seemed convinced that he'd called the wrong number in panic.

But Seth knew he hadn't made a mistake. He was

certain he'd selected *Mum* from his phone book. It was a day of accidents, bad luck, and total mystery.

The pain in Kim's wrist had become a relentless throbbing. Her stomach felt queasy and empty at the same time. She'd pulled her coat tightly around her, because she was shivering with cold. She was petrified that she would never play tennis again. Even as she drifted in a light sleep, her distress and suffering stayed with her.

When she shut her eyes, an image appeared in front of her. It was so lifelike, it could have been reality or a convincing mirage. She saw a young couple in a field, as clear as any of the patients in the waiting area.

The girl walked towards her, wearing a full-length linen dress, gathered at the waist. She moved noiselessly, almost seeming to glide. Her simple shoes were made of rough leather. She would have been very attractive, but her face was discoloured and her long dark hair was matted. The young man walking at her side was dressed in a worn jerkin, woollen gaiters and leather breeches. His boots were mud-spattered. His shirt was dull cotton and his shoulder-length hair was topped with a brimmed hat.

The vision seemed to consist entirely of shades of grey. The couple could have been the undead in an old black-and-white horror film. Unhurriedly, they approached Kim with terrifyingly blank expressions.

They were in their early twenties and the young woman looked even more sickly than Kim. Dark patches and black lumps tainted her neck and face. The two figures were very near now. Just a pace away and Kim could smell them. It reminded her of rotten meat. The couple stared straight at her, but still they remained silent. Then, without warning, the diseased girl stepped forward and held out her arms to hug Kim. Yet there was no affection in this embrace.

Awkwardly, Kim held her tender wrist out to protect it from agonizing contact. She flinched as the girl brought her face right up close. Her warm, foul breath enveloped Kim, who did her best not to gag.

The young woman did not withdraw. She gripped harder so that Kim could not back away. Then she leaned forward and planted a kiss on Kim's lips.

8

Kim jolted awake. The startling couple from her dream had gone. The first sight to meet her eyes was Wes, who had stirred suddenly at exactly the same time. And, like Kim, he was brushing his lips with his fingers as if he'd just received an unexpected kiss.

She stared at him, forgetting her injured wrist for

the first time, and said, "Did you just have a...a sort of dream?"

"Um. Yes. I suppose so," he answered, looking stunned and embarrassed.

"What happened?"

Wes shrugged. Reddening, he answered, "Nothing."

Seth looked from one to the other. "What are you two going on about?"

"I've just been kissed by... It's hard to explain," Kim answered.

Wes was staring at her with his mouth open. Even though he wouldn't admit it, he'd obviously had the same hallucination.

Kim jumped, as her flustered mother came up from behind saying, "You can't be too bad if you're thinking about kissing. Who kissed you? And what have you gone and done to yourself?"

"No one. It doesn't matter. I tripped over in class."

Mrs. Treanor squatted down in front of her daughter. "You poor thing. Let me see." She examined

Kim's wrist. "That's a nasty bruise and Seth said you couldn't move it."

Kim nodded.

"Hasn't a doctor seen you yet?"

Kim shook her head.

"I just went—" Seth began to explain.

Interrupting, his mum said, "I'll go and sort it out."

The doctor pointed at the negative and said, "There. See it? I'm afraid you've broken a bone. That's the bad news. The good news is, we can fix it and you'll be as good as new. At your age, the body repairs this sort of damage very nicely."

"Will I be able to play tennis?"

"Not tonight," he answered with a smile. "But you'll be back on court pretty quickly."

Painkillers – and the consultant's verdict – had dampened down the torment. Kim cocked her head, looked at the X-ray image, and rubbed her sore neck with her good hand. Strangely, she could feel the blood pulsing between her throat and ear.

The doctor stood back and then approached her again, saying, "Can I feel around your neck? It looks a wee bit puffed up to me."

Kim took her hand away and let him examine her.

"Mmm. Your glands are swollen. I'm going to put you on a course of antibiotics. Just in case you've got a bug of some sort."

Seth was pleased that he wasn't feeling ill as well. Not physically anyway. Most of Seth's pain was in his mind. He couldn't help thinking about the girl on crutches. If she was undergoing treatment in the Northern General, she'd probably be grateful to the hospital and she'd despise their heartless pilfering from Meadowhall. It was guilt and uncertainty that nagged at Seth.

* * *

The next day, Wes was hot and drenched with sweat at one moment, yet, a few minutes later, he'd be shivering with cold. He had a simple explanation, though. It must have been that water feature at Meadowhall. Seth had escaped the illness and he was the one who hadn't plunged into it. Along with Kim, Wes must have caught a chill in the shopping mall. Sent by his mum to see the doctor, he sat in the waiting room and scratched at the left side of his neck, where a reddened patch had begun to appear. He'd probably inflamed the skin with his fingernails. Then he rubbed both armpits and the tops of his legs.

When another patient tapped him on the shoulder, Wes removed the earpieces of his brand-new and expensive music player. "If you're Wesley Radcliffe," the old lady said, "your name's just been called." She pointed towards the surgery door.

Wes nodded and got up onto his aching legs.

He explained his symptoms and sat rigidly as the

GP's cold fingers probed the glands in his neck, armpits and near the top of both legs.

The doctor nodded knowingly. "You've got an infection. Antibiotics will put paid to it. That's what I'm prescribing." He waited for his computer to print out a slip, then he signed it and handed it over to Wes. "There. Three a day. One with every meal. But I want you to go upstairs to the nurse as well, so she can take a blood sample for tests. By the time we've got a result and identified the bug, the tablets should've shifted it anyway, but I'd still like to know what it is. For the record and in case of complications."

A quarter of an hour later, the nurse took his blood pressure, snapped on a pair of latex gloves and asked, "Are you squeamish about this at all? Seeing blood?"

"No," Wes replied, determined not to appear weak even though he was feeling sick before she began to examine his left arm for a vein.

She took the needle and murmured, "Let's see. This might do it."

It wasn't the confident manner that Wes wanted to hear as he felt the sting of the hypodermic needle piercing his flesh.

She found the vein at the third attempt. The crease in his arm near his elbow was looking like a messy pincushion by the time that she drew back the plunger, filling the syringe with his deep red blood. Before she finished taking the sample, she sniffed twice. Clearly anxious, she hesitated, breathed in deeply and then let out a huge sneeze. But she didn't let go of the syringe quickly enough. Her hand jerked it and the needle ripped through Wes's skin. The syringe fell to the floor and blood welled up from the ruptured vein and ran down his pale arm.

9

"Oh, dear!" the nurse cried. "Don't worry. Soon have you –" She grabbed a ball of cotton wool, slapped it on his wound, and lifted his forearm, so that his bent elbow applied enough pressure to stop the bleeding. "Sorry about that. I don't know... It's never happened before."

Overwhelmed by waves of nausea, Wes leaned

over the side of the chair to vomit.

By the time he felt clear-headed again, he had a plaster on his left arm and a neat little puncture in his right arm, where some blood had been sampled successfully.

In a moment of togetherness, Seth sat on Kim's bed at home that night. "It was a funny dream. You know, in the hospital yesterday." Kim sighed and trembled at the thought of it. "It was just a quick kiss. Hardly a big thing, but really creepy."

Seth listened as his sister described the two figures from bygone times and he felt sympathy towards her. Her wrist, encased in plaster, poked out from her sleeve, making it obvious that she wouldn't be troubling her tennis rivals for a while. Seth had imagined that frustration and illness would rage inside her, until she erupted like an angry volcano, spitting fire. But she'd become calm and thoughtful. Her eerie vision may have been low on drama, but it must have been high on impact. It had made her subdued rather than grumpy. Maybe the wait for the result of her blood test was also blunting her temper. In the meantime, the antibiotics didn't seem to be doing any good.

It was the same with Wes. Both Wes and Kim were going to be absent for the last three days of term. They were feverish for much of the time, and slipped in and out of sleep. They coughed and sneezed, complained about aches and pains, and often seemed hopelessly confused. They shivered and sweated in sequence. At least they didn't come up with any more crazy plans to raid wishing wells.

Having dull thumping headaches wasn't enough to get Seth off school as well.

"You know," Kim continued, "Wes had the same dream – or whatever it was. I could tell, just by looking at him. He won't admit it because he's all embarrassed about being kissed by a girl – probably enjoyed it. Weird, isn't it?"

Seth nodded. "More than weird."

"Some people say that sort of thing happens between twins. It should've been me and you, not Wes."

"Was the girl you saw on crutches?"

"Crutches? No, I don't think so. I didn't see any."

"Tomorrow, in school, I'll look a few things up," he told her.

"Like what?"

"Who the two people in your dream were."

Kim frowned. "How?"

"I was just thinking. Maybe they were Romans or people from when Eyam had the plague. I don't know. I could look up how they dressed."

If Kim had been feeling fit, she would have laughed aloud. She merely shrugged.

Seth was wondering if her hallucination was a faint echo of a Roman couple under a curse, or two people in Eyam whose lives had been torn apart by the Black Death. Or maybe the young woman who'd kissed Kim was the one on crutches. Kim's description sounded a bit like her, even if she hadn't noticed the crutches.

"Where did you put that Roman curse thing?"

Kim shrugged again, not because she didn't know, but because she was past caring. "Still in my coat pocket, I guess." She yawned. "Do you remember when we were little and one of us got sick?"

Seth nodded.

"When you were ill, I'd go down with the same thing. Mum'd be like, 'It's psychological – all in the mind. You're just trying to get in on the attention.' But it wasn't fair, you know. I was bound to pick stuff up from you. And twins are supposed to be finely tuned to each other, one feeling the other's suffering."

"Perhaps we did back then."

A sad smile came to her weary face. "I know these

days we don't...but... Anyway, I've heard you coughing. You might be like me in a few days."

"Yeah. Maybe." He gazed at her neck where an ugly bruise seemed to be darkening like the flesh of a rotting apple. "That's something to look forward to."

10

Later on Wednesday night, Seth went round to Wes's house. He found a ragged Wes sitting up in his bed, listening to music and playing with his Game Boy. But he looked droopy. He wasn't throwing himself into the game. It was just something to pass the time. Seth saw nothing of the friend who always hankered after excitement and action.

Wes seemed genuinely pleased to see him. He took out his earpieces and threw the game onto the blanket with a shrug. "My thumbs," he muttered with a sigh. "They don't work any more. Must be serious."

"How's it going?" asked Seth.

"Don't ask."

"That bad, eh? Like Kim."

"Don't be surprised if I get up and rush to the bog in a minute. Sometimes it's a toss-up knowing which end to point at the loo."

"Yuck."

"Are you catching it?"

Seth let out a long breath before he answered. "I don't know. I feel rough – like a cold or something – but Mum and Dad have prodded me here and there and say my glands aren't puffy."

Wes nodded and immediately winced at the pain in his neck. "You didn't go in the Meadowhall water."

"Yeah. But that's not all, is it?"

"How do you mean?"

Seth answered, "Maybe you caught something from that fungus – or whatever it was – off the old log by the pond. I said it was dodgy. Remember?" But Seth didn't really believe what he was saying. For one thing, he couldn't recall Kim touching the fungus.

"Maybe," Wes mumbled, unconvinced.

Seth decided to risk ridicule. "When you think about it, I didn't touch those two pieces of lead either. It was only you and Kim who handled them."

Wes didn't laugh. He thought about it for a second. "You can't pick up a bug from a lump of metal. Can you?"

"I don't know. I didn't dream about being kissed either. I don't suppose you can catch something from someone in a dream but –"

Wes gazed at him, probably trying to figure out if he was being serious. "That's crazy."

"When two people have the same dream at exactly the same time, you're in a crazy world. You did, didn't you?"

So far, Wes hadn't admitted to seeing the fantasy girl. Seth hoped that he would come clean now that Kim was out of range.

"It was...strange. I was in a field with a boy and a girl, a bit older than us. She was – you know – all right, but she'd got these sort of scabs." He brushed his hand over his cheeks and neck to show where the girl was marked. "She came up to me and... It was exciting and scary at the same time, if you know what I mean. She started kissing me. And, over her shoulder, I saw the bloke's face. He was... jealous. Yes, definitely. He didn't want her to kiss me, but he was eager as well. That's the thing I remember most. He was over the moon. Know what I mean? He stared at me like I was a slug for kissing his girlfriend, but he looked superior as well. Like he'd just hit the back of the net." He shook his head.

"How were they dressed?"

"No idea. I didn't notice. I remember he had a

stupid hat, that's all." He paused before adding in a croaky voice, "The whole thing's stupid."

"Maybe," Seth replied. But the more he learned, the more he believed in that faint echo of past lives. He suspected that the events of the last few days had something to do with a Roman couple blighted by a curse. Or it could be down to two people from Eyam, who'd been torn apart by plague. His mind went back to the message that Wes had thrown out. Maybe the couple in the dream was R.T. and Emma.

"I'll tell you what we should be worrying about," Wes muttered.

"What's that?"

He seemed annoyed. "I don't know where the money from the fountain's gone."

"The Meadowhall money?"

"Yes. Kim'll murder me. Did I give it to you or her? I thought... I can't remember."

Seth guessed that his confusion was part of the illness. "You didn't give it to me, no. I don't know about Kim, but I'll ask." He shrugged. "Didn't you say you put it under your bed?"

"Did I? Well, it's not there now. You check, just in case."

Seth ducked down and fiddled around underneath, moving the boxes and bags to get a good look. The dust that he disturbed made him cough. He got to his feet empty-handed.

Wes sighed and said, "It's nuts, but it's like it just melted away."

In the school library on Thursday, Seth found exactly what he needed. The internet search engine brought up far too many sites on clothing, but a handbook on dress through the ages was on the shelves. Flicking through its pages and looking at the pictures, though, he couldn't tell what fitted Wes's and Kim's description. He decided to borrow the book so that he could show it to them. That way, they should be able to use the identity parade of clothes to get a good idea who had paid them both a ghostly visit.

Seth was convinced that their shared vision was vital. It would have been interesting if just one of them had experienced an unsettling dream like that. It was extraordinary that they'd had the same fantasy at the same time. He believed it was his best clue for discovering what was going on.

Interrupting Seth's thoughts, Mr. Hanif asked after Kim.

"Her wrist's fine, thanks. It's patched up anyway. But she's off school because she's got some sort of infection." He shrugged.

"She's having a rough time. Give her my best wishes."

Seth nodded. "I...er...I've been meaning to ask."

"Ask what?"

"Why we throw things into water, especially coins. That guide in York said Romans threw lead curses into wells, and Brits used to chuck cut-off heads into the river. But why?"

Mr. Hanif smiled. "Good question. Everything's got a history. Did you know modern football's the result of kicking a sacrificial human head between villages? Throwing stones and coins into water's got a history as well. I doubt if it started with early Britons or Romans."

"What then?"

"No one knows for sure." Mr. Hanif hesitated and then said, "Archaeologists talk about ancient civilizations thinking of the sea or large lakes as a boundary between land and sky. I suppose that makes sense when people didn't understand the planet. A stretch of water – apparently with nothing beyond it but the sky – must have looked like the boundary between the worldly and other-worldly, if you see what I mean. That makes the edge of water a place to commune with the gods or the dead, I suppose, and offer them gifts. I know things like chariot fittings and weapons turn up in ancient lake beds. They were probably tossed in as gifts to the gods or to appease the spirits of the evil dead."

"Sort of makes sense."

"Yes. You can see how it could evolve into what we do today. If someone made an offering to the gods and the next harvest was a good one, it's like a wish come true. So, maybe we're conditioned to think throwing things – especially coins – into pools brings us good fortune. I know from my own kids, if you park them by a pond, they'll automatically pick up stones and chuck them in. It makes a satisfying splash when you're little, but maybe there's more to it."

"A hangover from making offerings to all sorts of gods," Seth replied.

"Precisely. Perhaps it's in our genes."

Seth thought about it for a moment. "Makes you wonder what the gods think of having their gifts nicked."

"How do you mean, Seth?"

He blushed. "Er...I mean, if archaeologists dig stuff up. That's like stealing the gods' gifts."

Mr. Hanif laughed. "You're right. They'd be pretty angry. Furious in fact. Well, you know what happens to people who break into tombs in the Egyptian pyramids."

"What's that?"

"Well, they say they're cursed. Some haven't lived long afterwards."

As Seth wandered over to Languages, he tried to count the number of people Kim and Wes could have upset by taking money from wells. The gods might have blessed with good luck anyone who offered chariot bits or coins, and damned with bad luck anyone who stole them, like archaeologists who took artefacts from the pyramids. There was John Hancock, who ran the city centre shop and whose family had lived in Eyam. Along with Wes and Kim, Seth had broken their promise to Mr. Hancock to take the message back to Mompesson's Well. There was also that girl on crutches and anyone who'd donated money to the hospital. All of them could bear the three friends a grudge.

Seth did not rule out R.T. and Emma from Eyam just because they were long since dead either. He wasn't sure he believed in ghosts, but plenty of people did. Maybe something could remain after death. Maybe lingering spirits could watch over the living or pester them pitilessly. If Emma and R.T. were the ghosts in Wes's and Kim's dream, maybe it was Emma who'd infected them through a kiss.

And Seth could think of another way that Kim and Wes might be haunted. Somewhere in York there had once been a Roman who'd put a curse on a cloak thief – or perhaps on all cloak thieves. That spell – to be crushed to a rotting corpse – might have transferred to Kim and Wes when Kim snatched it. Seth was particularly worried about that because Kim had bought a coat with stolen money. It was virtually a stolen cloak.

Seth was not short of candidates. He shivered as he realized how many people had a reason to be angry with them.

11

When Seth asked Kim about the money from Meadowhall Shopping Centre, she told him that she hadn't seen it. What's more, she didn't seem bothered by its disappearance. That was a first. Kim had always been rather fond of cash.

"Never mind," Seth said to her. "Take a look at this." He opened the library book on the history of clothing and put it in front of her. Then he turned the pages, while Kim gazed at the pictures one at a time. Whenever she seemed to lose concentration and drift to a different world, Seth nudged her. "How about this one? Did they look like that?"

"No."

Kim had lost the brightness in her eyes. And there was a sickly smell about her. Seth recalled the Eyam guide talking about the suffocating stench of death and he hoped that wasn't what was coming from Kim. It was unpleasant rather than repulsive. It wasn't a smell that made Seth flinch every time he took a breath, but it was there, niggling him. It wasn't upsetting Kim, though, because she didn't seem to be aware of it.

At last Kim stabbed a finger at a page of prints. "That's them!"

The page featured four images of typical clothing for a working-class family: a woman, a man, a girl and a boy. "Sure?" Seth replied.

"Certain. The hat gives it away. That's what the lad was wearing. And the woman's dress is what the girl had got on. More like a sack than designer gear."

Seth examined the handbook. The pictures were in a section called *Seventeenth Century Britain*. "Not Roman," he said. "It's in the sixteen hundreds."

"What does that prove?" asked Kim.

"Well," Seth said, "it's when Eyam was quarantined, because of plague. Remember our project? Sixteen sixty-something."

Kim stared at her brother. "Are you trying to tell me I got kissed by a four-hundred-year-old girl?"

Trying his best to lighten the mood, Seth shook his head. "No. Three hundred and forty."

When he went to Wes's house that evening, his mate picked out the same illustrations and the same brimmed hat. Running his finger across the image of the man, he said, "If he was younger, he could almost be the bloke I saw. The girl's different –

younger, not such a looker – but she's got the same feel."

"Kim picked them out as well," Seth told him.

"Creepy. Seventeenth century." Wes paused as if he was about to say something else but he didn't. He shrugged and scratched himself.

Seth was surprised by his lack of interest. "Don't you want to know what it means?"

"I suppose so."

Yet Seth could tell that he'd ceased to care. "I'll let you know. This," he said, tapping the book, "has pointed me in the right direction. I've got to do a bit more research on Eyam, because it looks like your dreamy people came from the time of the Black Death."

"Fair enough," Wes replied, casually.

"By the way, Kim's not got the Meadowhall money."

"I've been thinking," Wes said. "I was going to your place – to share it out – but I felt bad halfway and came home. Something like that, anyway. I don't remember bringing it back. I might've dropped it. Hope not."

Seth shrugged. "You've got more important things to worry about."

"Mum says the doctor's coming tomorrow. With the results of the blood test." He glanced down at the scabs in the crook of his left arm.

"Maybe I'll have some results as well," said Seth.

"What?"

"I might have worked out your dream."

At school on Friday, a gang of Kim's girlfriends stopped Seth at the top of the large stone staircase. "How's she doing?"

"Her wrist's healing as far as we know, but the bug –" He grimaced. "Not nice and getting worse. Parts of her are turning brown." He couldn't stop himself adding, "Like rotting flesh."

"Yuck. Is it catching?"

Seth shrugged. "She'll find out today. They've done some tests and she'll get the results this afternoon or tonight."

"We'd better not visit yet, then."

"Yeah. That's probably best." Seth paused before telling them, "Wes Radcliffe's the same. He's waiting for results as well."

A couple of them began to giggle. "What's Kim been getting up to with Wes?"

Seth grunted instead of answering properly.

"Maybe you've got it as well." They began to back away from him as if he were unclean.

"Very funny." As he turned away, his hand missed the banister and his foot slipped off the top step. His eyes opened wide in panic at the long drop that opened up in front of him.

12

The steps were made of brutal stone and Seth was about to bounce down a whole series of them before crashing onto the hard floor at the bottom. He'd be lucky if his only injuries were a few broken bones. In the instant before he pitched headlong down the unforgiving stairs, he tottered at the top with his arms wheeling.

It was that split second that saved Seth.

Behind him, a passing A-level student grabbed his rucksack and yanked him back from the edge.

Seth turned, his heart hammering in his chest. It took him two attempts to stammer, "Thanks."

The older boy smiled at him. "Look where you're going next time, eh? You owe me one."

Still shaken, Seth nodded. "Yeah. Sure." Then he repeated, "Thanks."

It was the last day of term, so Seth returned the library book about the history of clothing. It had served its purpose. It had given him a clear lead. Now, he felt sure that Kim and Wes had been visited in some way by a seventeenth-century couple. It was nothing to do with Roman Britain. So, he knew where to concentrate his efforts. After school, he nipped into town. Even though he felt uneasy about it, he returned to Hancock's Collectables.

As soon as Seth entered the shop, the dealer's face crinkled. It was clear that he was trying to recognize his young customer.

"Remember?" Seth said nervously. "Last Saturday. The coins from Eyam."

Mr. Hancock's frown disappeared. He smiled and nodded. "Ah, yes. Of course. The message on a piece of lead as well."

"Yes."

"What can I do for you?"

"I wondered if you knew anything about the people in Eyam at the time of the plague – you coming from there, in a way."

John shook his head. "I know about the Hancocks. That's all. There's lots of stuff on it, but I'm not a bookshop. You want the library. It's opposite the university." Then he hesitated and said, "Oh, it's Friday. They close early. Anyway, don't you young people ignore books and use the internet?"

Seth sighed. "I haven't got a computer and school's finished. One day, maybe."

"The money I gave you for the silver shilling must have helped."

"Yes. Thanks." Disappointed, Seth walked towards the door.

Mr. Hancock called after him, "Did you take the message back?"

Seth's hand froze on the door handle. "It's... er... tricky."

"Tricky? There's a bus goes from the Interchange up the road. Not that tricky. It doesn't cost an awful lot."

"I mean, Kim and Wes – my sister and friend – are sick at the moment."

John gazed at him in silence for a second. "Then it's time you kept your promise."

Was Mr. Hancock warning or threatening him? Seth wasn't sure. He shuddered and hurried from the shop.

* * *

Mrs. Radcliffe didn't know whether to feel relieved or alarmed. The doctor had delivered the result of Wesley's blood test and it was negative. Her son was not infected with anything. And that's why the antibiotics weren't helping. There were no known bugs in his body to beat. That was good news. But the doctor was no nearer to a diagnosis and an effective treatment.

"What are you saying? There's nothing wrong with him?" The stress in Mrs. Radcliffe's voice was clear. "Look." She lifted up her boy's bare arm.

Nestling in Wesley's armpit was a black lump that was almost the size of an egg.

"No. There's clearly something – especially because Kim Treanor's got the same symptoms."

The GP did not have to ask Wesley if the boil, filled with pus and blood, was painful. It was clear from his face, and the amount of sweat, that it was torture.

"I'll top up his painkillers," the doctor said, "but I think it might be time to admit him to hospital where they can keep a closer eye on him and perform more detailed tests." He paused and then added, "Let me go and see Kim Treanor first. Then I'll work something out for both of them."

Soon after Seth got up on Saturday morning, his twin sister and friend were bundled off to hospital. Seth was left alone at home with his brain full of outlandish theories involving sinister forces. He knew that Kim and Wes had upset the girl on crutches by stealing the hospital's money and John Hancock by not returning R.T.'s message. The shop owner's parting comment had even sounded like a threat. But Seth did not understand how either of them could be a cause of all the bad luck, accidents and disease. He suspected something spookier.

Seth was between Wes's house and his own,

making a dash for the tram, when he stumbled. He wasn't entirely sure what happened. Never a clumsy boy, he might not have been concentrating on where he was going. He might have been thinking too much about Eyam and how he could research its seventeenth-century inhabitants. Perhaps he tripped over his own foot or a ridge in the pavement. Perhaps the lad wearing a hoodie and going in the other direction caught his ankle by accident. Or even on purpose.

As he put out both hands to break his fall, Seth heard in his mind the sickening noise of Kim's wrist snapping. But he wasn't fated to suffer in the same way as his twin. The pain that would have started in his wrist and shot up his arm didn't come. There was no crack of bone. He heard another sound, though. That stupid nursery rhyme replayed in his head. *Ring-a-ring o' roses, A pocket full of posies. A-tishoo! A-tishoo! We all fall down.*

Flat out on the pavement, he felt only the tingly

sensation of grazed skin, and acute embarrassment. Three teenage boys pointed at him and laughed.

Seth was about to get to his feet with a grin and dust himself down, to show them that he could take a fall, when he noticed something hidden under the hedge. It was the same plastic bag that he'd used to collect the money from the Meadowhall water feature. He was astonished. If he'd walked past, he would never have spotted it. But sprawled on the slabs, he could hardly miss it. It was under the bush with some rubbish and decaying leaves, just beyond a nasty pile left by a dog. He screwed up his nose at the stench and carefully dragged the bag out. Straight away, its weight told him that the stolen cash was still inside.

Standing up, he looked around, trying to work out what had made him fall at this precise spot. It couldn't possibly be mere chance that he'd tripped over right by the carrier bag. Mystified, Seth shook his head and then glanced into the carrier bag.

At once, he felt ashamed. In some ways, he wished that the charity money had gone for ever, but it was back in his hands. It had returned to plague his conscience. He stuffed it quickly into his rucksack and continued into town.

13

Seth already knew a lot about the Eyam plague from his visit to the Derbyshire village and his own project, but he'd never taken in the names of the victims. In the public library, he booked a computer for half an hour and searched the internet for information on the unhappy episode. It didn't take long to find a website with all the detail he needed.

The Black Death came to Eyam in September 1665. The tailor's assistant, a man called George Viccars, opened a box of fabric that had just arrived from London. Unaware that rat fleas had hitched a ride to the Derbyshire village on the moist material, George shook the cloth and spread it out by the fire to dry. The fleas were teeming with the germs that caused the terrifying plague that was rampaging through London at the time. When a flea bit George, he did not realize that he would be dead in six days.

Set free in Eyam, the disease wasted no time. Before the end of September, six close neighbours had died. In October, the plague spread and took twenty-three more lives. Of the tailor's family, only his wife – Mary Hadfield – survived.

Many thought that the illness was a punishment for sin. They blamed a group of mischievous lads for bringing down God's wrath. The boys had driven cows into the church and the animals had fouled His holy place. Some villagers believed that the only cure was prayer and repentance in an attempt to win God's forgiveness. To seek any other remedy would be to make the sin worse in the eyes of God.

The village rectors, Thomas Stanley and William Mompesson, held services in the open air, making sure that each family group stood at least four paces apart. By closing the church and keeping the villagers at a distance, they hoped to stop the people infecting one another.

The rectors also persuaded the villagers of Eyam to take a pledge of extraordinary courage and heroism. They agreed to cut themselves off from the rest of England, so that they did not spread the plague beyond the village. If the sickness had reached the nearby towns of

Matlock, Chesterfield, Bakewell, Buxton and Sheffield, the consequences would have been unimaginable.

As the bible says, Greater love hath no man than this, that he lay down his life for his friends.

The people of the surrounding settlements left food for the villagers at the southern edge of Eyam and beside the spring that would later be called Mompesson's Well. In turn, the survivors put requests for supplies at the Boundary Stone. To pay for the goods, they placed silver coins in the well or in holes cut into the Boundary Stone. The running water in Mompesson's Well would wash away the seeds of plague, but there was no running water near the southern stone. Instead, they covered the coins in the holes with vinegar to cleanse them of the appalling disease.

Isolated from the world, the people of Eyam waited to live or die. A third of them died. The victims were buried quickly, without a funeral, in gardens and fields because the churchyard could not cope with the demand for graves. In one week of August 1666, poor Mrs. Hancock buried her husband and six of her seven children. But the villagers' sacrifice kept the plague and the stench of death within the confines of Eyam.

It seemed to be the same source of information that their tour guide had used. Seth even recognized some of the sentences. He also noted the awful fate suffered by John Hancock's ancestor. He read on eagerly until he found exactly what he wanted: a section on the experiences of individuals and families. William Mompesson, the rector. George Viccars, the tailor's assistant. More on Mrs. Hancock, who'd left Eyam after the quarantine and joined her one remaining son, who lived in Sheffield and worked in the cutlery trade. Mary Hadfield, the sole survivor of the tailor's family. Then there were three short paragraphs on someone called Rowland Torre.

A tingle ran down Seth's spine as he noted the boy's initials: R.T.

Each day of the quarantine, Rowland Torre walked the mile from Stoney Middleton to the edge of Eyam, where he had secretly arranged to see his fiancée. Throughout winter, when 1665 became 1666, he could look at Emmott Syddall from a distance for a few minutes. He could not touch her or speak to her. It was a poor substitute for contact, but at least he was comforted to know that she was safe. Yet, in April, she failed to show. Even though Emmott never again appeared at the village boundary, Rowland returned faithfully to the same spot every single day until December.

Seth caught his breath and his heart seemed to

stop. A mixture of excitement and shock surged through him like electricity. If R.T. was Rowland Torre – and he was sure he was right – then the name inscribed on the piece of metal was almost certainly Emmott, not Emma.

With Christmas approaching, Eyam was declared free of the Black Death and opened. Rowland was among the first to enter the village. He went directly to Emmott's home, but found it empty. Emmott had died eight months previously, together with her father and four of her brothers and sisters.

It is believed locally that a grief-stricken Rowland scratched a simple message of love on a tablet of lead and threw it into Mompesson's Well. It is said to lie there to this day. Superstition has it that there would be dire consequences for anyone disturbing Rowland's message.

The last paragraph confirmed it. It was right there on the screen. R.T.'s message of love, and dire consequences! Open-mouthed, Seth stared at it. Wes had exhumed an important part of Eyam's history. At the same time, he had stirred up old grievances and sorrow. And hatred. Rowland and Emmott would hate them for interfering with their precious token in Mompesson's Well.

Seth put his head in his hands, closed his eyes and shuddered. Why did he feel desperately sad for these people who had died over three hundred years ago? They were out of his experience and out of his reach. But it occurred to him that he might not be out of their reach. He believed that the spirits of Rowland and Emmott lingered in the present. Maybe it was because Emmott had suffered such a tragic and agonizing death. Maybe it was something to do with Eyam's sacrifice. Perhaps, it was because the quarantine, the plague and death had parted Rowland and Emmott before they could be married.

Why did Seth feel desperately frightened for his sister and friend? Even though it seemed incredible, Seth was certain that Emmott and Rowland had appeared to Kim and Wes in the hospital's waiting area. It had to be Emmott who had kissed them both.

And Emmott had been infected with the Black Death.

14

Seth decided that he had something very important to do at the hospital. Something even more important than visiting Kim and Wes. As the bus faltered through the stop-go traffic on its way to the Northern General, he gazed out of the window and wondered why Emmott had kissed the other two, but not him. Would she have kissed him if he'd been dozing like Kim and Wes? And if she had put her diseased lips on his, would he be suffering as well?

Maybe his imagination was working overtime. Maybe he was simply making a drama out of a few coincidences. That's what the others – his parents, the doctors, Kim and Wes – would claim, if he opened up to them. He had no intention of telling them what he thought, because they would never believe him. He would have to work out how to put things right himself.

Getting off the bus within sight of the main entrance to the Northern General, Seth halted. He delved inside his backpack, dragged out the bag of coins and then slung his rucksack onto his shoulder again. He plodded up the stone steps and crossed the ambulance access. As he approached the large doors, they opened automatically and silently for him.

When he entered the large reception area, he sensed that someone was behind him. He turned as he walked, glimpsing a lad in a brimmed hat. But

Seth's eyes must have been deceiving him, because the automatic doors slid shut behind him straight away. No one had followed him into the hospital. Holding the neck of the plastic bag tightly in his fist, he came to a halt.

To his right, a woman in a wheelchair tutted at his sudden stop and said, "Excuse me."

Seth said, "Sorry," and stood aside to let her through.

When he glanced around again, there was no sign of a young man wearing a hat or a hood. Instead, he saw a thin, bald man standing by the florist's shop with a green collecting bucket in his hand. The label on it read, *The Friends of Northern General Hospital.* That was perfect. Trying to forget the ghostly boy, Seth made for the charity worker.

The man rattled the money inside the bucket and held it out.

Without hesitating, Seth tipped up the carrier bag and emptied the entire contents into the bucket.

With a look of amazement, the man glanced inside to see a lot of extra cash, mostly pound coins. Astonished, he called after Seth, "Thanks. That's... very generous."

Seth felt better for giving the Meadowhall money to the hospital. He was following his conscience, but there was more to it than that. He hoped somehow it would help Kim and Wes. He couldn't believe it was coincidence that he'd fallen at the exact spot where Wes had dropped the bag of cash. To Seth, it seemed obvious that someone, or something, had guided him and, if he was right, there had to be a reason. He couldn't explain what had happened, but he wondered if Emmott Syddall and Rowland Torre were behind it.

At the entrance to the mixed ward, Seth had to clean his hands with an antibacterial wipe before he was allowed in to see his friend and his sister. The place reeked of antiseptic. At least it helped to cover up the whiff of decay coming from Wes. Seth let out a gasp when he caught sight of his mate. He was propped up in bed and his face was grey. Mrs. Radcliffe was hovering over him, clearly scared out of her wits. When Wes held a tissue limply over his mouth and hacked into it, the paper became spattered with deep red. Seth grimaced and looked away.

Around the corner, he found Kim in exactly the same state. She was letting out little groans, halfway between pain and tiredness. The bruised patches around her pale neck were now bulging and nearly black. One was oozing dark goo.

Seth swallowed, trying to be brave in the face of something shocking and unknown. Maybe Kim and Wes *had* caught a cold by getting wet in the Meadowhall water feature but, looking at the ugly outbreaks of dark swellings, he knew that their illness had been promoted to a different league. It was sneezes and runny noses that came from chills, not these horrendous blisters. Even their coughing wasn't normal. It brought up blood. Seth was certain that he was witnessing the dire consequences of disturbing Rowland's token.

Standing at Kim's bedside, while their parents took a tea break, Seth wondered if she'd been infected by Emmott's kiss or Rowland's lump of lead. He wasn't sure, but either seemed possible. While Seth had some aches and pains, perhaps he hadn't broken out in startling blotches or begun coughing blood because he hadn't been kissed and he hadn't touched the love token. He knew that no one should catch a disease from an imagined kiss, or from an ancient chunk of lead, but he feared that, somehow, the Eyam couple had got their revenge by infecting Kim and Wes with the Black Death. His next bit of research would sort it out once and for all.

Seth didn't tell either of them his theory about the illness, and R.T. and Emmott. Besides, they both seemed to be beyond caring about reasons and explanations. He could tell that they just wanted to be better. They just wanted to be normal again.

Leaning close to Kim, Seth said, "I forgot to tell you. Your mates asked about you yesterday. The tennis crowd as well."

"What did you tell them?" asked Kim.

"That you'd be back in circulation in no time," he lied.

"Huh. The hospital doesn't even know what's wrong."

"I'm going to find out," he whispered.

"Oh?"

"Yeah. I'm working on it."

She raised a pained smile. "Maybe it's your turn to be the crazy twin. You've waited long enough. I'm going to have to be the sensible one for a change."

Swallowing, to keep back his emotion, Seth nodded.

Seth went back to the library in the city centre. His skin began to tingle all over when he opened an on-line medical dictionary. The entry for *Black Death* told him that the disease had acquired its name from the dark bruises caused by bleeding into its victims' skin. The entry also gave Seth the alternative name of bubonic plague, and provided a link to the section on *Plague*. Seth's hand shook nervously as he double-clicked on the icon, because he already recognized Wes and Kim's symptoms.

There was a paragraph on how people became infected. Mostly it was about the fleas of black rats. Apparently, it was the bite of a flea that caused the disease in the first place. Then he read, with horror, that plague could be passed from one victim to another by coughing or kissing.

Symptoms of bubonic plague: aches, tiredness, vomiting, and coughing blood. Diarrhoea, fever and confusion. After a few days, buboes appear (acutely inflamed lymph glands). These extremely painful boils are filled with pus and blood. The dark blotches appear in the groin, sides of the neck, and armpits. They are one reason for naming the disease the Black Death.

Today, plague is a rare disease, because antibiotics control the infection, if taken without delay. There is also a vaccine that gives good protection if given annually. Before the development of modern drugs, plague was fatal in most cases. The bacteria moved to the liver, spleen and brain, causing bleeding and destruction, and demented behaviour. This behaviour lead people in the Middle Ages to regard the disease as the work of the Devil.

It was the final sentence that made his whole body shiver.

Death followed three days after the appearance of the black swellings.

15

Seth was suddenly certain that Kim and Wes were suffering from the Black Death. The symptoms were spot on. He was not just terrified by the prospect, but puzzled. He was a complete amateur, but he'd managed to figure it out, so why hadn't the hospital? And there was something else. It wasn't the Middle Ages any more. Seth knew that Kim and Wes had both been given antibiotics, so they should have been well on the road to recovery. According to the on-line dictionary, modern medicine had turned the Black Death into a rare disease, so why wasn't it helping them? Perhaps their version of the plague was the work of the Devil after all.

A voice in his head reminded him, *Death followed three days after the appearance of the black swellings.* He trembled at the thought. How long did that give Kim and Wes? He wasn't sure. He couldn't look at his watch and pin down an exact time when the horrible lumps had appeared. It wasn't like a gun firing at the beginning of a race, or the precise moment when Kim's wrist snapped. The bumps had emerged slowly. They had started as sore patches, slightly inflamed. Then they'd deepened to a red rash, like a "ring o' roses". Later, they'd darkened to brown-blue bruises, swelled hideously and turned a macabre black.

Seth thought he'd seen the first bruising on Kim's neck on Wednesday night. That was already three whole days ago. But he wouldn't have called it a black swelling on Wednesday night. Yesterday, though, she'd definitely got black lumps.

Then Seth remembered that the website on Eyam had given a timescale as well. The tailor's assistant had died six days after a fleabite had infected him. So, when had Kim and Wes been infected? It probably hadn't come from R.T.'s piece of lead, because Wes took it last Friday, eight days ago. But Emmott had kissed them on Tuesday night. Five days ago. That must have been the moment when they'd caught the plague! Emmott had given them a kiss of death.

Dazed by it all, Seth logged off. He had no reason to believe that Wes's and Kim's version of the Black Death – which didn't even show up in medical tests – followed the same rules as the real disease, but he guessed that he had as little as twenty-four hours to save Kim and Wes. Probably forty-eight hours at most. How could he make them better? Seth could think only of making it up to Rowland Torre and Emmott Syddall. Maybe, if he put matters right, their spirits would be satisfied without a death. Maybe they would spare his sister and best friend.

In a staff room at the Northern General, three members of the medical team drank strong coffee and scratched their heads as they discussed their most baffling cases. Dr. Twentyman took off his glasses and wiped his tired eyes. "Look. Someone's got to say it. Why aren't we stating the obvious?"

"What's that?"

They hesitated as a stroppy nurse walked through the group and opened a window, muttering, "It's too hot in here."

After she retreated to her seat, Dr. Twentyman replied, "We've got two cases of bubonic plague. Black Death."

The other two would have laughed aloud if it

hadn't been a serious matter. Lives depended on their decisions.

"Wrong. You know that's rubbish. The blood tests came back negative."

"I wish it *was* the plague," the third specialist said. "It's a doddle to treat with antibiotics these days. But these kids haven't responded to anything. It can't be the plague. No chance."

Twentyman nodded, but he wasn't beaten. "There is one way."

"Oh? What's that?"

"I talked to the parents. Both patients started going downhill about a week ago – after a school trip to Eyam. You know – the village that was hit by the seventeenth-century plague. Maybe, after all these years, the bacterium's learned how to resist drugs. It's become a superbug."

His colleagues gazed at him in amazement.

"It's no big deal," he said. "We all know bacteria develop drug resistance."

"If it was a school trip, why only two cases? And why those two?"

Dr. Twentyman shrugged. "We might get more. We'd have to isolate them. And isolate Eyam. Again."

The second doctor chipped in, "No. A drug-resistant form would explain why they're not responding to treatment, but you're still way off. The blood tests would have shown up a new version. No problem. Whatever they've got, it's not bacterial."

The third member of the team also rubbished Twentyman's idea. "Where's it been hiding all this time? Why pop up now? It doesn't make sense."

"I know. I know. It's a mystery," Dr. Twentyman said. "But, as far as I can see, I'm the only one offering any sort of diagnosis. What have you two got that's better? I reckon you need to come up with something today or tomorrow. If I remember my history right, the Black Death was fatal about a week after infection, and three days after the buboes turn black. Monday might be too late. By then, we might be explaining to the parents why we lost their kids."

The man outside could not believe what he was hearing through the open window. He'd been visiting his brother in the cancer ward, but the strain of it all had got too much for him. He'd gone out for a smoke before he could carry on the act of being positive and cheerful in the face of a cruel condition. On the lawn outside, he'd leaned against a fire exit, lit up, and taken a deep and satisfying drag on the cigarette.

It was then, even before he'd finished expelling the first stream of smoke, that an astonishing story drifted out of an open window. "We've got two cases of bubonic plague. Black Death," a voice said. The man held his breath, keeping the smoke swirling around his lungs, throat and mouth, as he listened closely. It was almost unbelievable but some doctors were discussing the possibility that bubonic plague had returned to Eyam.

He dropped his cigarette onto the grass and stamped on it. Despite the pain of his brother's illness, a smile lit up his face as he walked off. For a reporter, he'd just had an amazing stroke of luck.

The nurses hadn't let Seth back into the ward because, they said, the patients needed to rest. Seth had gone home with his mum and dad. But that night, he couldn't sleep. There was too much thinking and planning to do. He had to bring the run of bad luck to an end. He had to make amends. And he could think of only one way of doing it.

If Rowland Torre and Emmott Syddall were punishing Wes and Kim for removing their love token, Seth might be able to appease them by keeping the promise to take it back to Mompesson's Well, where it was meant to rest for ever.

In the darkness of his room, Seth wondered if Rowland and Emmott had spared him because he'd tried to persuade Kim and Wes to return the message. But maybe it was simpler than that. Maybe he hadn't been haunted – and cursed with the Black Death – because the Eyam ghosts needed him in good shape to replace the lead in the well.

The first thing Seth needed was that symbol of love. As early as possible the next morning, he would have to ask Wes where he'd put it. Seth was sure that Wes had said something about throwing it away, but he couldn't remember where.

Eventually, the rising sun made his curtains glow and he heard the newspaper plop onto the mat in the hall. Shortly after, there was uproar. Seth dressed and dashed downstairs to see why his mum and dad were going spare. They were both staring at the Sunday newspaper. Shocked silence alternated with frantic exclamations. The cause of their distress was clear. It was written in huge bold letters on the front page.

PLAGUE AWAKENS IN EYAM?
TWO IN SCARE AT SHEFFIELD HOSPITAL

16

Seth's mum was as white as a sheet. He'd never seen her so scared. And his dad was fuming. He wasn't sure if they were panic-stricken because Kim might catch the plague while she was in the hospital, or because they suspected that she was one of the two victims.

Trying to find out, Seth asked, "What's up?"

His mum simply looked terrified. His dad passed him the newspaper and said, "Sorry, Seth. You'd better read this."

The article was very thin on detail. There was nothing about Kim and Wes. Most of it described the horrifying history of the plague in Eyam. Hardly news. Clearly, the reporter had heard a rumour and attempted to pad it out to make an attention-grabbing article. Bold subheadings read: *Possible drug-resistant form* and *New Eyam quarantine proposed*. It was more about scaremongering and selling newspapers than informing readers.

Most people wouldn't take any notice of the question mark in the sensational headline. They wouldn't believe the official denials, either. They would see only the return of the dreaded Black Death.

"Is that our Kim?" Mum shrieked. "Is that what she's got?"

Dad looked helpless. "I don't know, love. But

we're going to the hospital to find out." He made a dash for his coat.

Seth said, "I'll come."

There was a swarm of journalists and a camera crew outside the main entrance of the Northern General. The Treanors slipped in through the side door next to the Physiotherapy Department and hurried down endless corridors to Kim's ward.

While the twins' mum and dad went in search of an explanation from the nursing staff, Seth visited Kim first and then Wes. The hospital hadn't quarantined them, because every test was still negative. Logic demanded that they could not have the Black Death. But they both looked terrible.

What struck Seth most was their awful colour. Apart from the seeping black boils, they were a lifeless grey, like the faces of zombies in films. And everyone knew that zombies were already dead.

Kim was throwing herself madly from side to side, like someone demented. When Seth appeared beside her, though, she quietened to the point of barely stirring at all. Seth wasn't sure which was worse. At least when she thrashed around, she was clearly alive and fighting. He hoped that a period of calm didn't mean that her body had given up. She did not react to his quaking voice.

Wes was not quite asleep and not really awake. He showed no sign of hearing Seth. Even so, Seth had to try. He didn't have a choice. While a nurse was within hearing, he kept to small talk. "Mr. Hanif's given us an extension on our Roman project, by the way. It can wait till you're better, till next term."

When the nurse moved away, Seth lowered his voice and said, "I've worked it out. I think I can save you and Kim." He looked around to make sure no one else was listening. "It sounds mad, I know. You can't catch anything from kissing a fantasy girl, but... I'm sure I'm right. You got the plague from R.T. and

Emmott. They want that piece of lead – their message – back. I can take it. Just tell me where you put it."

The only sound that escaped Wes's lips was an inhuman groan.

Seth grabbed his arm and squeezed. "Where is it, Wes? You've got to tell me!"

Wes opened his eyes, but Seth could tell that he wasn't seeing anything in this world. Even if Wes had felt up to talking, he was probably too confused to tell Seth anything that made sense. He shook off Seth's hand and, like Kim, began to toss from side to side as if possessed.

Feeling wretched, Seth stepped back and shook his head. Without the Eyam message, it was impossible to help Wes or Kim. No doubt, the doctors and nurses would rush around with pills, tubes, liquids and creams, but Seth was convinced that only the lump of lead could save them. He left his parents at the hospital and took a bus to Wes's house.

The place was deserted. By now, Mrs. Radcliffe

was probably at the hospital herself. Like Seth's mum and dad, she'd be sobbing, screaming or silent.

Seth could not even search Wes's room for the love token. With heavy legs, he trudged round to the back of his friend's house and plonked himself down on the fallen log, beside the stagnant pond. In the farm opposite, the cows were all ambling towards a ramshackle shed. The scene reminded him of what he'd read about the Eyam plague. Some villagers had blamed a bunch of boys, because they'd driven cows into the church, angering God. Seth let out a long breath and then coughed into his hand. He examined his palm and fingers anxiously, but there was no sign of blood.

Gazing at the pond, he thought again of how their misfortune had begun. Wes and Kim had taken advantage of everyone's habit of throwing coins – and other things – into water. It was an appealing tradition. Whenever Wes came here, he always threw stones into the pond. Now, Seth fished around in his pocket and found a ten-pence piece. Desperate enough to try anything, Seth drew back his arm, tossed the coin into the water and made a wish. He wished that Kim and Wes would get well.

But he didn't really believe a simple wish was enough. He had to return the lead token, but how was he ever going to find it? Almost at once, an idea came into his head. If R.T. had guided him to the right spot to recover the missing charity money yesterday, maybe Rowland had already worked the same magic again. Heart pounding, Seth jumped to his feet. The last time he'd been to this spot with Kim and Wes, they'd sat together on the old rotting log, chatting about the two pieces of lead. Suddenly, Seth recalled exactly what Wes had said. He'd grumbled about the love token. "It was horrible to touch and it really hurt where it rubbed against me. Made me feel terrible so I chucked it."

Seth stared at the grubby pool. Knowing what he had to do, he took a deep breath and grimaced.

17

Crossing the rough ground, skidding on the wet soil, Seth made for the water. At the edge, he hesitated and surveyed the pool. He'd always been told to keep away from water like this. He had no idea how deep it was. It could be dangerous. But he had the lives of his sister and best friend to save. He took a step forward and his foot slipped away from him.

To stop himself from pitching forward and getting a complete soaking, he threw himself deliberately to the side. Both hands squelched into the soft earth and one of his feet ended up in the pond. Scrambling upright again, he looked down at his shoes and clothes. One foot was dripping foul water already and the other was a heavy mass of mud. His trousers and coat sleeves were stained a horrible brown colour. "Yuck," he muttered. Then he shrugged, sneezed, and stepped cautiously into the shallow water.

It would have been natural for Wes to aim for the centre of the pond when he hurled the chunk of lead. Normally, his aim was good, so that's where Seth decided to begin – as long as it wasn't too deep for him. He waded slowly towards the middle, planting each foot carefully in the silt, so that he didn't fall over. The sludge at the bottom and the water itself seemed to be dragging at him, trying to stop him, but he carried on warily.

When he got to the centre, the water was above his knees. To touch the sediment with his hands, he'd have to plunge his arms into the cold, smelly water right to his shoulder. The pool was far too filthy for Seth to see anything beyond the first few centimetres so he'd also have to dredge the slime through his fingers, blindly.

Bent over, arms dipped deep into the pool, Seth shivered. It was horrible. He could imagine finding all sorts of revolting things, or having his hand bitten by unseen fish. For all he knew, there could be discarded needles, or knives, lurking in the mud. Or a human skull. Still determined, though, he dragged his freezing fingers through the slushy stuff at the bottom. His first four finds were all stones. He might have thrown them there himself. Or Wes or Kim could have chucked them in.

As he continued to delve into the mud, he stirred up more of a stink. He didn't look down into the pool. That was pointless. Rather, he kept his chin up as much as possible and his face turned away.

His hand came into contact with something solid and metallic. With an expression of disgust on his face, he pushed his fingers deeper into the mire, to get underneath it, and then prised it upwards. It came away with a sucking sensation. At the surface, crud fell away from it, revealing a cheese grater. Seth turned up his nose and let it sink again. He didn't have the time to wonder why someone had thrown a cheese grater into the pond. He was in a race to find and return R.T.'s message, before Kim and Wes lost their lives.

Next, he scooped up an old videotape. Out of the water for the first time in ages, the cassette oozed mud like thick brown blood.

Under every one of Seth's fingernails, there was a black arch of dirt. He frowned, discouraged, but not yet ready to give up.

After discovering a milk bottle, two more stones and half a brick, Seth touched something small and heavy. This time, it seemed to be the right size and shape, slightly smaller than his palm. He wiggled his fingers in the mud to penetrate further down. His mouth and cheek were forced perilously close to the surface as he reached lower. He could easily imagine the dirty water flooding into his nose and mouth, into his throat and stomach. He grimaced with the stench, the effort and the nausea.

The object came free of the sludge with a sucking sound. As soon as he straightened up and got it near the top of the water, he smiled. It was the familiar piece of lead, with a trail of goo leading back into the depths. Relieved, Seth washed it underwater, by rubbing it between his palms as if it were a small bar of soap. Then he waded back to dry land as quickly as he could.

His light-headed feeling of triumph soon evaporated as he gazed at his catch. Kim and Wes may not have developed the plague symptoms until Emmott had kissed them, but they'd both suffered aches and pains after coming into contact with this token of love. Wes had even complained that the lead hurt him. It occurred to Seth that he might now succumb to the same feelings.

He needed to make for Eyam as quickly as he could but he was a complete mess – drenched, dirty and dripping – and he was out of money. He was also shaking uncontrollably. He decided to warm himself by running home, where he could pick up enough money for the tram and bus fares, and change his clothes. At least his parents wouldn't be there to ask a lot of awkward questions.

He would have liked to take a shower but he didn't want to waste time. Instead, Seth scrubbed at his hands and fingers fiercely, as if he were trying not just to get clean, but to eliminate the memory of his dip in the mucky pond. Then he stripped off hastily. While he slipped on clean jeans, he came across a bruise at the top of his left leg. His fingertips froze on it and his heart stopped for a moment. The mark was exactly where the lead had rested in his trouser pocket. Maybe it was natural and inevitable, because the heavy chunk of lead might have banged against his skin as he jogged home. Or maybe he'd picked up the injury at the pond and it was just coincidence that it was by his pocket. But Seth imagined there was more to it.

He wondered if it was possible for people to think themselves into serious sickness. To get out of double science, it was easy to come up with the idea of a dreadful toothache – and then begin to feel it in reality – even though there was nothing for a dentist to fix. It was all in the mind. Whenever Seth had any sort of illness that kept him away from school, Kim always thought she deserved equal treatment. She used to convince herself that she'd caught it as well. But Seth knew there was no way his twin could make herself come out in pus-filled boils. She wasn't *that* good at faking. Even so, his idea would explain a lot. No amount of powerful antibiotics would make the disease go away if it was all in the mind, put there by an angry Emmott and Rowland.

Seth just hoped that he wasn't now thinking himself into the plague. The stain on his leg was real – and the bruise hurt when he pressed it – so he found it difficult to believe that his brain had concocted it. Even if it was the beginnings of the Black Death, there was no point in going to a surgery or hospital. The doctors couldn't cure it with their pockets full of modern posies. They couldn't even detect it. Perhaps that was because they were looking in the wrong place, with the wrong tools. The disease was beyond their clever science and beyond medical tests.

"Come on," Seth told himself aloud. "Emmott didn't kiss me and a bruise is just a bruise. It's nothing."

He didn't convince himself, though. He imagined

that it was a reminder of his duty to Rowland and Emmott.

Scrambling into the rest of his clothes, Seth looked again at the piece of grey lead that lay in his palm. Wes was right. It felt chilling and uncomfortable – as if it were much more than a dull lump of metal. The old scratchy message had turned it into an important symbol. It belonged only to victims of the plague. And if it weren't returned to them, maybe it would bring down the illness on its new owners.

Swallowing nervously, Seth slipped the token back into his trouser pocket. As he made for the door, the flesh of his hand stung where his skin had been in contact with the lead. He felt as if he'd been cut with a knife.

Kim could no longer tell the difference between dreaming and reality. She thought she'd heard Seth and her mum, but she couldn't recall seeing them. She was certain she'd seen the seventeenth century couple again, but she couldn't recall hearing them. Quite often, they stood silently at the end of her bed – more real than her own living twin – and waited with empty expressions. The doctors' visits to her bedside had ceased to make an impression on her. She knew only that they'd started to talk about her as if she weren't there at all.

She was living her life against a background of pain and incredible cramps. Her heart felt hollow and weak. It also seemed to Kim that some cruel torturer had invented a way of blowing up her skin so much that it was on the point of bursting like an overstretched balloon.

Sometimes, the shabby young man in the hat drifted from the foot of her bed to her side and appeared to be examining the bleeping machines and tubes that dripped water and nourishment into her body. With a curious look, he'd put out his hand as if he were going to drag one of the tubes closer to himself.

Kim would start to cry, "Don't pull it out!" but the plastic would pass right through the lad's fingers and barely move.

Without a sound, he'd return to the girl who had kissed Kim.

Kim began to cry. She might have been overwhelmed by her own condition, it might have been her endless aches and pains, but it could have been sympathy for those two strange people, who gazed into each other's faces with such undying love.

18

By the time Seth got off the tram and walked to Sheffield Interchange in the city centre, he was feeling sick and faint, but he knew he had to be strong. The lives of his sister and best friend were in his hands. If he was wrong about R.T.'s message – or if he was right, but failed in his attempt to return it – there was little hope for Kim and Wes. He was also convinced that he'd share their fate if he didn't fulfil their promise. Resisting the temptation to go back home and take to his bed, he made for the Derbyshire village.

It was a small single-deck bus that pulled into the bay. He got on and asked for a return ticket to Eyam.

The driver leaned towards the clear plastic screen that separated her from the passengers. "Sorry?"

"Return to Eyam, please," he said loudly.

"Eyam?"

"Yes."

"I'm not calling there."

"But I thought... Is this a number sixty-five?"

"Haven't you heard?" the driver asked.

"What?"

"About the plague. I've got three kids. I'm not taking the plague home with me."

Realizing that she must have read the newspaper article, Seth nodded. "Eyam's not been cut off, has it?"

"No," she answered impatiently. "The powers-that-be say there's no problem. Like people are going to believe them! It's not worth the risk. My union says I don't have to stop there if I'm worried."

"Can you drop me as close as you go?"

"I suppose so. I wouldn't go at all, if I was you."

Seth paused, not knowing how to reply. He certainly wasn't going to mention his inside knowledge. And he thought trying to persuade her that the village was safe would be a waste of time. "I'll...er...I'll take my chance."

"All right. The nearest stop is Stoney Middleton."

Seth let out a little gasp. He recognized the name at once.

Each day of the quarantine, Rowland Torre walked the mile from Stoney Middleton to the edge of Eyam, where he had secretly arranged to see his fiancée.

Seth would have to follow in Rowland's footsteps to return his message.

"Are you all right?" the driver asked. "You look a bit –" She hesitated and, in an attempt at humour, added, "I don't want you pegging out on my bus. It'll inconvenience the other passengers."

Seth couldn't raise a smile. "I'm fine," he fibbed as he reached for his wallet.

The driver pulled up at the bus stop on the main road through Stoney Middleton. "There," she said, pointing across at the other side of the street. "Up that lane, there's a footpath to Eyam."

Seth muttered, "Thanks." Normally he jumped down from a bus, but this time he stepped down gingerly on sore legs. Now he knew what Wes had meant when he said that the token made him feel rotten.

He watched the bus accelerate into the distance, bypassing the Derbyshire plague village, and then he crossed the road.

The driver was right. A few metres up the lane, there was a stile and a wooden signpost, pointing north across an open field where sheep were grazing lazily. *Public footpath. Eyam. 1½ mile.* The trail was unmistakable, because it was a deep green strip through the paler grass on either side. Seth didn't fancy it, though, because it sloped steeply upwards. He took a deep breath and pulled himself up and over the stile.

As soon as he began to trudge up the grassy rise, he realized that his footwear was unsuitable. He'd put on ordinary shoes, because his trainers were saturated, but the soles didn't provide enough grip. The ground was greasy with mud and a strong cold wind blew down the hill against him. Every time he took a step forward, his trailing foot slid back awkwardly. Soon, sodden clods of earth stuck to his shoes, hindering him.

The sheep barely moved, even when he went quite close to them. They must have been used to tourists heading for Eyam. According to the website, it was only a mile from Stoney Middleton to the boundary of the village. According to the signpost, it was only a mile and a half to the centre of Eyam, but already it felt like a marathon. And Seth remembered that he had to walk at least another half a mile beyond the village to reach Mompesson's Well. That track was steeply uphill too.

His legs were aching already and pain gnawed at his hip. The chill air stung his throat and made his lungs throb. The lead in his pocket felt cold and, like his shoes, it seemed to be three times its normal weight. Perhaps it was warning him against giving up, dumping it somewhere near Eyam, and going home.

His arms and head began to feel like lead as well. But he didn't dwell on the thought. He had no time to regret his own worsening health when, for all he knew, Kim and Wes could be on the point of death. He had to crack on.

Stepping out, both shoes lost their grip on the slippery soil. He plonked a hand down on the ground to stop himself skidding backwards. Once he'd steadied himself, he stretched and began to stagger forwards and upwards. As he went, he thought of poor Rowland Torre, walking this route every day in the dark winter months of 1665 and 1666.

Eventually, the gradient lessened and Seth stopped to get his breath back. On the high ground, he felt the full force of the wind. His eyes watered as he looked ahead to see a disused farm and then the small cluster of houses at Eyam. Just beyond the village, the land became wooded and rose again. That was where he had to go.

On his right, off the main track, there was a solitary boulder. It looked unremarkable at a distance, but a minor path led to it. Drawn towards the stone, Seth realized what it was as soon as he saw the six holes cut in its flat top. It was the Boundary

Stone, where the survivors placed silver coins in vinegar to pay for supplies during the quarantine.

Seth's school party hadn't visited the stone, because it was too far from the other side of the village where most of the historic sites lay. Seth peered into the holes in the boulder. There was nothing in them now but rainwater. He wondered how many times Rowland had taken cleansed coins from here in payment for goods from Stoney Middleton. Each time, he must have thought about his Emmott and wondered whether he would ever touch her again.

The main path narrowed. Now, two drystone walls hemmed in the track. It wasn't just mud underfoot any more. There were rough rocks and large puddles. Seth ploughed through it all. He wiped his dripping nose on his hand and passed sideways through one of the tight gaps in the walls. After negotiating another of the cracks, he turned his face towards the village again and gasped. Some distance ahead of him, he saw a young woman in old-fashioned clothes, standing at the head of the lane that ran into Eyam. She seemed to be waiting for something. Or someone.

Overhead, a huge sheet of cloud blotted out the entire sky and darkened the Derbyshire moor.

19

Wes was in a fever. He thought he was standing beside Kim. For some reason, he seemed spellbound, unable to move. Opposite them stood the old-fashioned couple. The young woman who had kissed him faced Kim. Her boyfriend with his brimmed hat stood in front of Wes, gazing fixedly at him. Anyone watching would have thought the four of them were playing mind games. But no one was watching. At least, Wes didn't think so. Everything seemed to be happening in a void. Wes saw nothing beyond the bizarre couple.

The young man was pale to the point of being grey, but at least he didn't bear the ugly blood-filled boils that littered the girl's face and neck. Wes couldn't define the expressions on their faces. At one moment, they were merely sad. Sometimes, it was anger and malice.

Slowly, the silent and menacing figures lifted their arms towards Wes and Kim. The lad's arms stretched out towards Wes and the young woman reached for Kim. Their shared gesture was odd. They almost seemed to be welcoming Wes and Kim into their world, to the world of the dead.

Seth frowned and screwed up his eyes, squinting at the solitary figure. Then something made him look over his shoulder, back towards the Boundary Stone. Way behind him, there was the dark shape of a boy in a hat, barely more than a silhouette.

Seth turned again and the walls either side of him appeared to spin. Stone and shadowy shapes whirled past him. In those few seconds, he appeared to be surrounded and trapped. The dizzying effect made him woozy and sick. But eventually the world around him came to a halt and he tried to focus on the way ahead again. The image of the young woman had gone. And there was no one behind him either. He was alone.

Swaying unpleasantly, he put out a hand and grasped the top of one wall, steadying himself before he felt able to walk in a straight line. Taking a deep breath, he let go of the stone and continued along the trail. Soon, he passed the spot where the girl had been standing.

Seth squeezed through a gate and entered the narrow lane. A couple of minutes later, he emerged into the village square that he recognized. To his left, a television crew was interviewing someone. On the other side of the main road, there was a butcher's shop next to a small café. Before, when he'd wandered past with the school party, he hadn't noticed that the butcher's was called *George Siddall*. He guessed that the owner was a descendant of Emmott Syddall's family. He crossed the road and looked briefly through the window, but the shop was closed. After all, it was Sunday afternoon.

He glanced up at the sky, worried that he was about to be caught in a downpour. But there was nothing he could do about it. If the rain came, he'd have to put up with a soaking. Refusing to surrender to misery and self-pity, he turned to the right and hurried along the street for a short distance, until he reached the footpath that he wanted.

A signpost marked the start of the track through the bleak wood. This time, the distance wasn't written on the pointer. It read simply *Mompesson's*

Well. As far as Seth could remember, it was a tiring twenty-minute walk up a rough path. He recalled the teachers shouting warnings to be careful because, near the top of the trail, there was a very steep drop down to a stream on the left-hand side. It hadn't been scary at all in a school group. But this time, on his own, feeling dizzy, with dark cloud hanging just above the treetops, the mood was very different.

At first, the well-worn track wove through the wood, rising gradually. Underfoot, it was mud with rocks and tree roots. Seth had to be careful where he put his feet, but the way was easy. Step by step, though, the path changed. The gradient increased and he entered a dense collection of firs. Here, it was totally quiet. The closely packed trees deadened the atmosphere. Seth heard only his own heartbeat and footsteps. And the trickling of the stream in the gorge.

Seth could feel the bruise at the top of his leg as he walked. The token in his pocket knocked against it and the rough lining of his trousers aggravated the bruise. The contact was infuriating.

He began to struggle as the uneven trail led steeply up through the wood. His lungs on fire, he gasped for breath as he climbed, slipped and slid. The relentless ache in the joints of his right leg sapped his strength. He was tired to the point of exhaustion, but he couldn't allow himself to stop and turn back, defeated. Sometimes, he grabbed a tree trunk and clung to it for a minute. While he recovered a little of his strength, he kicked at the air in an attempt to dislodge the earth from his shoes but, each time he tried it, he nearly fell as his other foot skated on the slippery soil.

His heart thudded as he looked over the precipice at the side of the footpath. It was almost a sheer drop to the small river a long way below. At once, he looked up and took a deep breath to stop himself feeling faint.

He grabbed at another tree and hauled himself a

few metres further towards the road at the top of the hill. Ahead of him, a brook crossed his path and plunged over the edge of the valley to feed the stream. Deliberately, Seth stood in the flowing water to rinse the mud from his shoes and reduce the weight that he was carrying. It helped a bit, but he could do nothing about his other two burdens. He was sore – suffering more and more as he strained every muscle. And there was the lead in his pocket. As he dragged himself up the slope, it felt as if he were carrying a sack of potatoes.

Seth's head was fit to burst. His brain was not making clear sense of the world any more. He imagined that R.T.'s lump of lead had a mind of its own. He had thought – and hoped – it would help him reach Mompesson's Well, but there was no sign of it easing his way. Quite the opposite. In Seth's confusion, he thought that the love token was punishing him. He guessed that it wanted him to suffer. And he guessed that Rowland Torre was testing him. He looked around in case the angry ghost was hiding in the trees, watching him. This time, he saw no one, but the firs seemed to sway and crisscross each other, as if they were closing in on him.

Seth staggered back. Perilously close to the edge, his right foot slipped on a wet root and he toppled.

Feeling the mud give way under him, he landed on his knees and slid towards the sheer drop. His numbed legs went over and his chin crashed against the edge of the sludgy bank, banging his teeth together painfully. Breaking the silence of the wood, he screeched in fright and threw out a hand in a desperate attempt to clutch at anything solid.

20

It was the stump of a tree that saved him. He had one hand on its rough bark, supporting the weight of his dangling body. He wasn't thinking at all any more. In panic, he acted solely by instinct. He flung his other arm around the remains of the tree and hung on for his life.

Taking a few more gasps of air, he began to pull

himself up, trying to get a grip on the unstable bank with his feet and knees. As he tugged, his stretched arms felt as if they were on the point of tearing. As soon as his scrabbling legs found a firm ledge, he pushed against it and inched closer to the footpath and safety. But the combination of soil, moist moss and leaves gave way and he slipped back.

Refusing to admit defeat, he locked the fingers of both hands around the trunk and used the remaining strength in his arms to heave himself slowly up towards the verge. When his shoulders came level with the footpath, his left foot lodged on a rock poking out of the bank. With a secure toehold, he could pause for a moment and gather himself for one final effort. Hugging the tree stump, he tensed his arms and shoulders again and thrust against the stone. Bashing his battered knees into the bank and finding one more solid grip for his foot was just enough. He yanked himself back onto the trail and rolled away from the edge.

Flat out and finished, his fogged eyes saw the silhouettes of upper branches against the grey cloud overhead, and then nothing. He passed out with pain and fatigue.

Minutes or hours later, he was roused by a voice. "Nearly there," it said. Strangely, it must have been his own voice, because there was no one else around. Opening his eyes, he was surprised that it was so dark. Perhaps it was the effect of the mist drifting through the sinister wood, or maybe it was dusk.

Seth could barely feel his right hand and his feet. They prickled horribly with pins and needles. He got to his knees and then used a branch to pull himself upright. He felt dreadful, but at least he hadn't plunged down the chasm. Thankful, he took a few steps and found it surprisingly easy to totter onwards. Automatically, his hand went to his pocket and he realized why he was not feeling so laden. The lump of lead had gone.

Drained, he let out a long, weary breath and

groaned. He wanted to give up, to leave Eyam and this filthy wood. He wanted to go home, flop onto his bed, and wake up fit and well. He'd got rid of R.T.'s message and he felt much better for it. But he couldn't turn back now. He would never be fit and well until the lead token was restored to its rightful place. And he had yet to save Kim and Wes – if they were still alive.

He went back to the lip of the bank where he'd fallen. The place was obvious, because his thrashing legs had churned up the soil. Squatting carefully by the verge, he peered down the gradient.

And there it was. He could just make out the piece of lead nestling on a tuft of moss, supported by an exposed root. But it was beyond his reach.

He looked around for something that would help. A long branch. Then, before he lost light altogether, he went back to the same spot with it. He lay down on the track so that his head, shoulders and arms jutted out over the drop. Reaching down, he manoeuvred the tip of the branch carefully, so that it was just beyond the small metal plate. Then he scraped it upwards until he nudged the lead onto a higher root. He adjusted his grip on the branch and then did the same again. Bit by bit, he dragged the token closer and closer until it was within arm's length. Then he dropped the branch, reached down and grabbed R.T.'s piece of lead.

It was so icy that it hurt. He imagined that, if he held it for more than an instant, his skin would freeze onto it. He dropped it into his pocket as quickly as he could and then blew warm breath onto his hand. Even in the gloom, he could see that his skin was red and rough where he'd touched the metal.

He was running out of time. The fog and the night were closing in. Rowland's message was itching to be home as much as Seth needed the comfort of his own house. As fast as he could, he struggled up to the top of the trail. Leaving the wood behind, he joined the road. It was lighter in the open, but the whole area was shrouded with cloud. There was not even the reassuring sound of cars and the sight of headlights searching. The road was quiet and deserted.

If it had been a clear, moonlit evening, he would have been able to see the sign to Mompesson's Well beside the lane. In this shadowy world, he could see little. As he stumbled towards the site, he thought he saw someone standing at the side of the road, pointing silently at the well. He was too tired and hurt to hurry or to smile, but he felt relief that he was nearing his goal.

As he approached the way to the well, the swirling mist fell away from the ghostly figure. Seth's muddled mind had mistaken it for a tragic figure from the past, but it was merely a signpost. He turned off the lane, staggered the few steps over meadowland to the well, and sank onto his knees.

In front of him was the stone hood that covered half of Mompesson's Well. The rest was open to the air, like an outdoor washbasin. If it hadn't been so dark, he would have seen some coins glinting at the bottom.

He was frightened to grasp the lead with his bare hands but it had to be done. Summoning the last of his courage, he delved into his pocket. He caught his breath in astonishment when his numbed fingers closed around a warm and smooth piece of metal. Shocked, he pulled it out into the open and took one last look at the message lying in his palm. This, he hoped, was the answer to Wes's and Kim's illness.

There was no time to lose. He looked up into the fog for a moment and whispered, "Emmott, true love always, rest in peace, R.T."

He plunged his hand with the token into the well. Now, the water felt colder than the metal. Seth didn't let go of it straight away. He searched for a spot where the bank overhung the stone well. That way, the lead could lie out of sight and undisturbed. Stretching downwards, Seth placed it carefully in the right-hand corner.

His skin came away from the metal and a warm tingle spread throughout his sore body. At once, he knew he had done the right thing. He hoped that Rowland and Emmott would now forgive them. He prayed that the ghostly couple would wash away the seeds of plague that they'd planted in Wes's and Kim's minds, just like the spring water of Mompesson's Well and the vinegar in the Boundary Stone had cleansed coins many years ago.

He expected that, somewhere, Rowland Torre and Emmott Syddall were now satisfied.

Seth got to his feet and dragged himself back towards the lane. But he didn't have an opportunity to work out how he'd return to Eyam, Stoney Middleton and Sheffield. Shattered, he collapsed at the side of the road.

21

Seth came properly to his senses on Monday morning. When he finally managed to keep his flickering eyes open, he realized that he was in hospital. His mum, dad and a nurse were peering at him.

"Are you back with us?" his mum asked anxiously. "Are you all right?"

"Um –" He was groggy, but he felt no pain. Under the sheet, he felt the top of his right leg. There was no sign of a swelling. His uncertainty turned into a smile. "I'm fine."

"You looked like you'd been dragged through a hedge," the nurse told him. "Cuts and bruises, but we didn't find anything else. We can discharge you as soon as you feel up to going home." She glanced at his parents and back again. "But you might have some explaining to do."

"You're not kidding," his father exclaimed.

Keen to hear about his sister and friend, Seth asked, "How are – ?"

His dad cut him short. "What were you doing in Eyam? A bloke spotted you collapsed by the side of the road."

"A bloke?"

His mum explained. "A Mr. Siddall. He said he was the village butcher, driving home after a weekend away when he saw you and picked you up.

You owe him a big favour."

Seth got up on his elbows and nodded. It was Emmott's descendant who had helped him.

"But what were you doing there?" his dad asked again, his relief replaced by irritation. "Your sister and Wes are suffering no end and you go walkabouts to Eyam. What were you thinking of?"

"It's a long story, Dad."

His father shook his head. "That's not good enough, Seth."

"How are they? Kim and Wes."

"You're not going to fob me off—"

A flustered Dr. Twentyman interrupted them. "Mr. and Mrs. Treanor," he said hurriedly. "I need to speak to you. There's been...a development."

Kim thought she should still be in bed, but she seemed to be standing in the aisle alongside it. A motionless Wes appeared next to her. Opposite them stood the bizarre, old-fashioned couple. Facing Kim was the young woman who had kissed her. The lad, with his strange hat and muddied boots, stood in front of Wes, gazing fixedly at him.

Kim felt as cold as the grave. She imagined this was what it was like at the boundary between life and death. This was the moment she'd been dreading. Or maybe it was just another dream, but it seemed real.

Kim brushed her neck and face with her hand. She knew that she had bleeding sores just like the pale young woman. She knew that she had also become ugly. Letting her hand fall, Kim tried to interpret the expressions on the silent couple's faces. There was sadness, but no menace.

Slowly, the two of them lifted their arms towards Kim and Wes. The young woman reached for Kim and the lad's arms stretched out towards Wes. They seemed to be welcoming Kim and Wes into their world.

Kim shuddered. She wanted to turn and run but she was too poorly and terror fixed her to the spot. The diseased girl walked up to her and showed no sign of stopping or sidestepping. In parallel, the lad walked beside her, about to bump into Wes.

Kim braced herself.

But the collision did not come. The strange woman seemed to step inside her, just like the young man's hand had once gone right through one of the tubes at her bedside. Kim spun round. The tragic girl appeared behind her and the lad passed right through Wes. Together, the ancient couple walked away into the world of the dead. While Kim watched them vanish, as if into a fog, the deep chill that had gripped her was replaced with a luxurious warm tingle.

After his endeavours, Seth thought that Kim and Wes would have recovered magically. But he was being too optimistic. Kim was lying in the bed, unaware of anything around her. He could still recognize her as his twin, but her exposed skin was covered in a black and red rash, ruining her appearance. Seth's heart pounded, because he thought he had failed.

But he hadn't.

Kim stirred and Dr. Twentyman looked delighted. "I know you can't see much of a difference but, believe me, *we* can. Her symptoms started to ease last night. Her temperature's dropped to something like normal. These swellings on her neck have stabilized. Some have gone down. None of them erupted in the night and there's no new ones. She even took a sip of water this morning." He smiled at the family. "Don't ask me to explain, but there's hope for her now. And Wesley's the same. Our medical mysteries have become medical miracles."

Only Seth understood why the disease was loosening its grip. Only Seth understood why they were both on the road to recovery.

22

Four days later, it was Good Friday. But Kim and Wes didn't know that. To them, the passage of time was a blur.

Seth waited until his parents went to speak to the nurses, before he whispered, "You're looking great. Well, in comparison with what you were like. Both of you. Anyway, I know what happened. I took R.T.'s message back. You know, to Eyam."

Sitting on the other side of Kim's bed, Wes looked puzzled. "You couldn't," he replied. "I threw it in the pond. Unless you –"

Seth nodded. "I did, yes. And now you're a lot better."

"But that's –" Still flat out, Kim seemed to be on the point of rubbishing the idea that their illness had anything to do with the Eyam plague, but she stopped.

Seth beamed at her. "You believe me, don't you? They were called Rowland Torre and Emmott Syddall, not Emma."

Kim gazed at him for a moment and then returned his smile. Suddenly, they each knew what the other was thinking for the first time in years. "Yes. I'm pleased for them," said Kim.

Missing out, Wes asked, "What are you two talking about?"

"Seth did it," Kim answered quietly. "Emmott and Rowland are satisfied. They walked away. It was nice. Peaceful. They're at rest. Like their love token."

* * *

Soon after Easter, Wes and Kim were discharged from the Northern General. The medical team had not solved the riddle of their illness before being equally bamboozled by their return to health. "I guess," Dr. Twentyman said, "getting you well again is more important than a diagnosis, but..." He shrugged for the hundredth time. "Maybe one of the drugs we tried worked after all."

Mrs. Radcliffe arrived first and took Wes away.

When Mr. and Mrs. Treanor turned up, Kim wrapped herself in her new coat, before she faced the outside world. Seth watched her shove her left hand deep into the pocket and frown for an instant. She lifted out her fist and glanced down as she opened her hand. On her palm was the Roman curse. She smiled wryly, shook her head, and put it back in her pocket, out of sight.

For an instant, Seth caught his breath. He'd forgotten about the curse from York. But he didn't have to worry. Their bad luck was down to the events at Eyam. Nothing to do with Romans. He shrugged at her.

"Got all your stuff?" Mr. Treanor asked her.

Kim nodded.

"Come on, then," Mrs. Treanor said with a wide grin. "Home."

The main doors sprang back as the family walked out of the hospital. Mr. and Mrs. Treanor led the way. Seth and Kim shuffled along behind, not speaking, but closer than they'd been in ages.

Their parents had crossed over the emergency access road by the time Seth and Kim reached it. Seth could tell that Kim was emotionally calm at last. He put his insight down to the intuitive bond between twins. He also knew that she was still thinking about the couple who had been parted by the Black Death and the Eyam quarantine three hundred and forty years ago. She was so absorbed in her thoughts that she didn't see the ambulance speeding round the corner.

When Seth came to an abrupt stop at the kerb, Kim kept on walking.

"No!" Seth cried, making a grab at her coat.

His fingers touched the material, but he didn't manage to get a grip and yank her back.

Kim heard him, maybe felt him, because she turned. But, with a look of absolute horror on her face, she stumbled. The front corner of the ambulance slammed into her, spun her round and tossed her aside. Her scream and the squeal of tyres became one dreadful sound until everything went very quiet. Her twisted body crumpled horribly.

Seth dropped to his knees and clutched at his sister's arm. "Kim! Kim!"

Her eyes shut tight, she did not reply. Her left leg lay at an unnatural angle, her other limbs were splayed in all directions. A little blood was dribbling from her nose and mouth onto the double yellow lines at the edge of the narrow road.

Bent over her, Seth didn't know whether to touch her or not. She was uncannily still. When he sniffed back tears of anguish, he was overcome by a dreadful smell. It seemed to be a combination of burning rubber and decaying flesh.

Chaos kicked in. Hospital staff and the twins' parents were running towards them. But Seth didn't notice. All he saw was the York curse lying on the tarmac. It had spilled from Kim's pocket. And he remembered the awful words of the spell:

He who wears another's cloak will be crushed to a rotting corpse.